THE LAST MEDIUM

Dark Covenant Series Book 2

DEAN RASMUSSEN

The Last Medium: Dark Covenant Series Book 2

Dean Rasmussen

For more information about this book, visit:

www.deanrasmussen.com
dean@deanrasmussen.com

The Last Medium: Dark Covenant Series Book 2

Published by: Dark Venture Press

Cover Art: MiblArt

❋ Formatted with Vellum

AUTHOR'S NOTE

Readers should be aware that Chapter One contains a scene involving harm to animals as part of a ritual. Those sensitive to such material may wish to skip that chapter or keep this in mind before continuing.

❧ I ❧

Gabriel switched off all the lights in the house and crossed the living room toward the massive fireplace. It filled an entire wall. When he'd purchased the home, he hadn't thought he would ever use the fireplace, much less rely on it. But now it seemed indispensable. The house was old, with a Victorian charm—something his daughter had loved—but the oversized firebox seemed almost excessive. It was huge, and well-used, judging by the blackened stones along the bottom. He'd hesitated to bother with having someone clean it when they'd moved in. Why clean it if he would never use it? But now he was glad he had done it.

The fire had started without any problems. The flames crackled inside the hearth, surrounded by a circle of candles he'd arranged on the floor in front of it. He'd meticulously placed them with all the care of a medical procedure, following the instructions exactly. There was no margin for error.

He'd left the note on the nearby couch, where he'd curled up with his dogs so many times. There was no chance that the ones who discovered him would miss it.

It wasn't his home anymore, anyway. Those days were gone. Everything had changed when Anna had died. Ever since her passing, he'd existed in emotional darkness but had come to embrace the emptiness. It had awakened a part of him he had never listened to before—a still, small voice at the back of his mind, reminding him he could still do something about his loss. He wasn't powerless. This wasn't the end. He didn't need to accept reality on the world's terms.

There was another way.

He'd discovered he could still reach his daughter while also delivering retribution to those who'd taken advantage of his grief. Everything could be made right if he just committed himself.

The branding iron hissed as he lifted it out of the fire. The tip glowed orange as he stepped toward his four pets—his children—who lay "asleep" on the floor. They were not really asleep, of course. He had given them sedatives. No need to make them suffer, too. It was just as he'd done so many times before in his office for his clients' pets. Only this time, it wasn't an act of healing, but of sacrifice.

It was all about love and care, but in a different form. He could take them with him. His entire family together again. Forever.

He stepped over to the German shepherd first—Rosie. Just a puppy when Anna had received her as a "birthday present" on her third birthday. Anna had named her Rosie because she'd smelled like roses—the breeder mentioned washing all the puppies beforehand.

Gabriel pressed the red-hot branding iron into Rosie's side, marking the spot carefully, pressing harder than necessary—to be sure. There could be no doubt about his intentions. Rosie twitched and gasped even in her drugged sleep. A moment later, it was done. The seared flesh was beautiful in a way—a permanent reminder, an agreement, a binding contract to the one waiting for them in the darkness. It was a signal to the spirits— Rosie was ready.

Three more to go.

He went to the second dog, a pit bull named Atlas, and did the same. He didn't press the branding iron into Atlas with as much force. He couldn't. Atlas didn't wake, but he stirred. Gabriel's heart ached at seeing his blind, aging rescue dog twitching and spasming involuntarily. What was going through the animal's mind? Was he consciously aware on some level of what was happening? But any suffering would end soon.

Moving along to the third, a Doberman pinscher named Nero, he did the same. Nero was an abused rescue dog, and his most loyal friend. Barely a shudder from him as the iron's tip seared the mark into his flesh, although it had cooled a bit since he'd started.

He went to the cat next, Blanco, and pressed it against his flesh. The cat twitched just like the others, but also his back arched slightly as if he teetered on the edge of waking up.

"It's the only way, Blanco," he whispered. "It won't be long now."

Moving on to the next step in the ritual.

One last sacrifice—himself.

He took off his shirt and stood bare-chested in the heat of the raging fire. Without hesitation, he pressed the branding iron against his chest with both hands, forcing it into himself as deep as he could manage. A fresh wave of pain ripped through his mind. His scream tore through the house—echoing up the stairs, through the hallway, to Anna's room. Had she somehow heard his cry from her throne in heaven?

Struggling to stay conscious, he forced himself to continue.

Taking out his pocket knife, he turned the blade against his palm and slashed a line across his skin without hesitation. The sting was sharp but sweet in that moment. The pain seemed to bring him a little closer to Anna.

As the blood welled up, he brought his hand over to the first dog and let the blood drop into its fur near their wounds. He started chanting. He'd memorized the words beforehand, and now his practice paid off. The Latin rolled off his tongue in a rhythmic tone. He was doing everything just as instructed. Finally, he repeated the words in English, to say them from his heart:

"This I give you, my Moloch, all I have—my child within this fire, to prove my faith in you." A tear flowed down his cheek. "I relinquish my sight to take on immortal eyes. To see through the darkness to the gift that awaits me—my daughter, Anna."

Moving to the next dog, he did the same, letting the drops fall a little faster now.

When they'd all received his blood, he stepped back. There was no reaction. Not yet. He wasn't finished.

He lifted Rosie first with care and reverence. He carried her to the edge of the fireplace and lowered her into the flames. The stench of burning fur and flesh filled the room, and smoke thickened the air.

With the fire consuming the first dog, he stepped over to the next. Kneeling beside Atlas, he scooped him up and carried him to the edge of the fireplace. Lowering Atlas with as much care as he could manage, he placed him on top of Rosie's carcass. A flash of heat swept over Gabriel's face. The flames whooshed higher, and he turned back to complete the next task.

Nero was next but lifting him was a struggle. The pinscher was larger than most, and his weight nearly broke Gabriel. Carrying him the last few steps into the open fireplace, he heaved him inside with a loud gasp and added his cherished Nero to the pile.

Stepping back, he watched the flames dance. They surged higher for a moment, until something shifted within the fireplace. The flames crackled louder, and something tapped against the side of the firebox like a nervous tick—Nero's paw?

Just involuntary muscle twitching.

The sound grew louder before it stopped.

"It won't be long now, my children," he said. "We'll be together again soon."

With his gaze still fixed on the flames, he reached back to grab Blanco.

But his hand met empty space.

The cat was gone. Had the sedative worn off too early? He rarely miscalculated such things, but it was possible. Working backwards through the process in his mind, Gabriel realized his mistake. He *had* checked the dosage twice, but he hadn't seen the numbers clearly through his tears. Eight and three had looked the same in his trembling hands. It didn't matter. Blanco couldn't have gotten far—all the doors and windows were shut.

Still, panic swept through him, and he forced himself to focus. He took a moment to step through in his mind everything he'd done so far. He'd sedated the cat like the others. He'd carefully measured out the doses for each animal based on their weight. It was enough—more than enough—to put them to sleep, but not enough to kill them. Moloch demanded a living sacrifice when it touched the flames.

So where was the cat?

"Blanco..." Gabriel called out, peeking behind the couch. "Come here, boy. I've got something for you. A mission. A sacred duty."

Silence.

Blanco must have awakened from the sedative early. He *had* sedated Blanco first, and the process had taken longer than expected. He'd paused in front of each dog to say goodbye. Maybe too much time had elapsed during those sentimental moments. Or maybe the hot iron had jolted the cat's system back to consciousness.

If so, he could be anywhere. He might be hiding beneath the furniture, seeking shelter in his carrier, or upstairs in a closet. Or maybe he'd lapsed back into unconsciousness after lumbering away from the fireplace and finding refuge in some dark corner. The implications sent Gabriel's temples throbbing.

"Blanco, don't run from me... Not now. Not after everything I've done for you. All the years I fed you and cared for you. You want to do this for Anna, don't you? This is all for her. For us. To be together. This is the only way. Come back to me. One last time."

Footsteps broke the silence—a soft pattering sound from the next room.

He was in the kitchen. At least, he was alive.

"Here kitty kitty," Gabriel said in a desperate whisper.

Another meow came from just around the corner.

"Yes," Gabriel said. A flood of relief swept through him. "I knew you wouldn't leave me. There you are. You understand, don't you? This isn't the end. We're just going to a new home—a better place. Anna is waiting for you, Blanco. You'll see her too."

Another meow—though this time, further away.

It was coming from near the back door.

He'd closed it, hadn't he? He wasn't sure anymore. When had he brought the dogs inside for the last time? They had swept around him with such force while rushing inside that... he hadn't heard the latch click, and he hadn't bothered to check.

Gabriel lurched forward. He had to move faster if Blanco was to join the others.

Stepping softly into the kitchen, he moved around the kitchen table and followed the soft sound of Blanco purring. Not so much a purr as a watery rasp. The sedatives hadn't completely worn off yet. The kitchen counter was just ahead, the fridge to the right, the back door to the left. He hadn't gone far, but there was still no sign of him. Had Blanco instinctively headed toward the back door to be let out?

"We're not going out, Blanco." Gabriel reached the door and gripped the handle. "Not this time."

The door floated open. It was unlatched, and the sound of paws scampered past him. Before Gabriel could react, Blanco's tail brushed against his leg, and the cat swept through the open door, slipping out into the night.

"No, Blanco!" he cried into the darkness. "Don't go! Don't leave me!"

But it was too late.

"I'm sorry." His shoulders drooped. "Please forgive me, Moloch. I gave you all of my children—they are yours, all that I have. Please forgive the one that escaped. He is marked and still belongs to you."

Still, he couldn't stop now. There was more work to do.

Arriving back at the fireplace, he moved on to the next step of the ritual while the flames still consumed his pile of sacrifices.

Lifting a knife off the floor—the one his guide had provided, the one carved from bone—he held it up toward the flames, its blade gleaming in the flickering glow. His hands trembled, but he didn't hesitate. This was everything he'd prepared for. The sedatives had dulled his body, but not his resolve. Everyone had betrayed him—everyone except Moloch.

Turning the blade toward his left eye, he began carving into the tender flesh around his eyeball. He severed the muscles first, then the veins that held it in place. The pain exploded through his brain and nearly brought him to his knees. Struggling to stay conscious, he tore the left one free and let it drop to the floor.

As blood spilled down his cheeks, warm and oozing, he moved on to the right side. He clenched his teeth to keep them from rattling. The agony tore through him in waves—worse than anything he'd ever experienced. For a moment, he almost passed out. He was sure his skull might burst through his ruined eye socket.

The right eyeball popped out next with a sickening slurp, and the world went black forever.

A strange peace swept over him. Despite the fire roaring in front of him, he was cold—chilled to the bone. Blood seeped into his mouth. He didn't bother to spit it away—it seemed to nourish him, to provide a little comfort. The nightmare would be over soon.

"Are you here, Master?" Gabriel said into the darkness. "Are you proud of me?"

Stumbling back, he grabbed at anything for balance. It was

difficult to breathe. His sinuses were flooding, and he was on the verge of passing out.

"I won't give up... the memory of everyone who betrayed me..." He clenched his jaw as the pain intensified. "I won't forget."

Trudging forward with the last of his strength, he stumbled after only two steps and then collapsed. Writhing on the floor, his bloody eye sockets throbbed with a hellish fire like someone had injected lava into his brain. The sound of the flames crackling in the fireplace faded into the distance, and the stench of burning flesh filled his nostrils.

"Wait for me, Anna," he said with chattering teeth, his mind slipping into darkness. "No rest for the wicked."

❦   2   ❦

"This is the last of it," Father Tony said. He came out of the back room carrying a cardboard box and set it on the kitchen table. He opened the flaps and started lifting things out one at a time, laying each piece on the table with a little more care than necessary. "This is all the stuff I couldn't quite figure out. I didn't have the heart to toss it in the garbage. I didn't have the guts either."

Each object he unveiled stirred Ally's curiosity a little more. There were a few old books like others she'd seen from a previous visit, but these seemed a little older, a little more worn. He placed the fragile items together in a cluster: a blackened bundle of sage bound in rusted wire, a thin velvet pouch sealed shut with wax, and a glass orb that reflected her wide eyes like a giant marble.

One of the books was hand-stitched, and Father Tony opened it with care, pausing on a few pages while turning it to face her. One page was filled with scribbled passages in what looked like Latin and Greek, along with some twisted shorthand filling the margins. Some of the pages were charred along the edges, while others were stuck together. She recognized a few of the symbols that repeated again and again, although she didn't remember from where—one that looked like an inverted chalice, one like a goat's eye.

He didn't comment on the content. Just a glimpse of what was inside—enough for her to draw her own conclusions.

In the end, Father Tony paused when he reached the bottom of the box. Half buried in crumpled paper, he pulled out a wooden box, roughly the size of a shoebox, made of what looked like mahogany. The edges were scorched and a little warped, as if it had sat too close to a fire but had survived anyway. Someone had replaced the rusted metal latch with a crude loop of wire. Father Tony didn't open it.

"This is the one I was talking about," he said. "I know you're curious, like with everything else, but I need you to let this one go. You can't keep it. Do you understand?"

Ally didn't touch it, but the symbols etched across its surface sent her imagination racing. "What's inside?"

Father Tony exhaled like he'd been holding his breath for days. "It's sealed."

The sigil carved into its lid looked like a hollow flame split down the center, like it had once been whole. She reached for it instinctively, but Father Tony pulled it away.

"Promise me you'll dispose of this," Father Tony said. "I've tried, but it doesn't burn. Not in the fireplace, not even when the kindling hissed like it wanted to swallow it. I fished it back out of the embers a few hours later. The fire made no difference."

"I promise," she said softly. "I'll take care of it."

"Keep it away from Blanco. He's at Nora's house, correct?"

Ally nodded.

"That's good," he said.

"Why should I keep Blanco away from it?" she asked. "He doesn't like it?"

"Something like that. Just having it around... It seems to irritate him. Maybe the smell reminds him of what happened."

Before she could get a better look at it, he wrapped the

wooden box in an old blue towel frayed at the corners and taped it shut—twice. Placing it reverently inside the cardboard box, he packed everything around it, then taped that shut as if trying to bury it.

"I can see the way you're looking at these items," he said.

She turned and met his gaze. "Of course, I'm curious," she said with a little laugh. "But I'm not scared."

Father Tony didn't blink. "You should be."

A moment of silence passed between them.

"What was Gabriel trying to do with it?" she asked. "The old box, I mean."

"Gabriel believed it was a key. He said it had ties to Moloch, claimed someone had instructed him—someone he never named. A mentor, in a sense. Or a guide. After all the failed attempts to contact Anna, this was his last resort. He stopped listening to me after he got this. He stopped listening to anyone."

Ally nodded.

Sealing up the box, he nudged it toward her. "I can carry it to your car."

"I got it," she said. "And I *will* destroy it when I'm done."

Father Tony's hand shot out, touching her wrist with surprising strength. "No. Do it *now*. *Today*. Not after you've taken your notes and satisfied your curiosity. Destroy it, or bury it, or wrap it in chains and drop it in the middle of a lake. You can keep everything in here... except the box. Pretend you never saw it."

She didn't answer right away. "I understand."

Father Tony followed her all the way to the door without speaking, and only after she had stepped outside on her way to the car did he call out. "I trust you."

She nodded without turning back, and he shut the door between them.

The late afternoon air was warm and breezy. A perfect day to go to the beach or take Lucy to the playground. But these items would keep her busy for at least a few days as she researched their significance.

She placed the box gently onto the back seat as if afraid of breaking anything inside. Even through the cardboard, she could still smell the scent of burning wood—the smell of Gabriel's twisted obsession to contact his daughter in the afterlife. This was the last remnant of his venture into the darkest corners of the occult.

And it belonged to her now.

She started the car and headed out onto the street on her way back to the parlor. Daniel and Nora would be waiting for her, expecting her to return with nothing more than dust and junk. How could she explain the importance of what she had in her backseat? It was better that she didn't let them see what she was bringing inside. Something like this would just make them nervous anyway.

Of course, she would dispose of it and keep her promise to Father Tony when the time was right. But the thought of throwing that mahogany box into the lake, forever buried beneath a layer of weeds and silt, nauseated her.

She couldn't just let it go so easily. Not yet. Not until she understood what it meant. Not until she knew what Gabriel had almost discovered.

Nora stepped away from the wall, wiped the sweat from her forehead with the back of her wrist, and set down her paintbrush. Tarps and painter's tape covered everything. The parlor was a far cry from what it used to be, but the changes were somehow thrilling. She could see through the chaos to what she and her sister had envisioned months earlier: to transform the House of Vale into something more *true*, to shift away from her father's incessant push for deception and greed. Now they had a new mission statement, one that Nora had printed out and framed on the wall next to the front desk: "No tricks. Only truth."

She'd given up performing séances and had even stopped dyeing her hair black—something she'd done at her father's request. Its natural color, a dark brown, was finally resurfacing after years buried under the black dye. Its return felt like rediscovering an old friend.

Never again—her Madame Lenora persona was finished, although Ally would continue offering the séances in a more ethical way. Nora had seen the dark side of her actions and what her lies and deception had nearly cost them. Ally was in charge and would handle every aspect of their psychic business from now on. Her sister had a genuine knack for all that, anyway—something *real*—and her college background in folklore, the occult, and spiritualism would take center stage, instead of manipulative theatrics in the séance room.

They were just switching places. Nora would handle everything up front—greeting the customers, scheduling, and leading any guided meditations or grief support sessions. Those were the things she really cared about anyway—helping grieving individuals move on.

It wouldn't *completely* change. They would offer all the same services as before—the séances, the astrology charts, the palm readings, the tarot card readings—except everything would go through Ally.

The changes might rock the foundation of House of Vale. Maybe they would lose a few clients, but they might also gain some new ones. They were still a psychic parlor dabbling in the occult—just without all the nonsense their parents had trained them to do. It was a fresh start.

Nora stepped back and glanced around the parlor. The atmosphere was somehow different—hopeful—without all the fake theatrics.

Lucy's small voice rose above the silence every few minutes. She was playing with Blanco somewhere in the back.

The money for the renovations had come unexpectedly. Ally had discovered it in their father's apartment after his death, tucked away in a battered box at the back of his closet, marked with nothing but three cryptic Xs. Inside were old stock certificates, some yellowed with age, some dating back decades. He'd been quietly investing behind their backs, hiding away a small fortune while the rest of them scraped by, worrying how they'd even afford to keep the lights on for another month.

The shock of it hit hard. At first, there was disbelief, then anger—at how easily he'd lied, how convincingly he'd played the part of a man with nothing. The certificates were worth nearly a hundred thousand dollars—enough to finally make things right with the business. It would buy them some time. But the money came tainted. It didn't feel like a gift. It felt like the last trick in a long line of betrayals.

He'd raised them to believe that truth was dangerous, and survival meant never showing your hand. And now, in death, he'd revealed the biggest deception of all: their lives, their struggles, had been carefully constructed fictions. All those years of going without, of watching their mother worry, of feeling like they had to earn every scrap of peace—they were built on a lie.

At least Daniel was there to help. He'd taken a short break from his regular Maintenance Technician job at the school, just as Lucy's summer break had started. He was stretching to paint a hard-to-reach area near the ceiling in the front room. After she paused and looked around, he turned back to her. "Where's Ally? Isn't she coming in today?"

"She went to pick up some things from Father Tony's house."

He grimaced. "Again?"

"This should be the last of it," Nora said.

"The closet's stuffed with your family's things we still haven't sorted through yet. How much stuff is that old guy giving away?"

"It's not his stuff," Nora said. "Father Tony needs our help. Gabriel left behind some unusual items—things he can't just drop off at a donation center."

"Then toss it in the garbage," he said.

Nora shook her head, even though he wasn't looking at her anymore. "It's not trash. Some of it is dangerous—we can't let it fall into the wrong hands."

"Then burn it."

She smirked. "Ally's taking care of it. She can deal with it better than anyone else. It won't take her long."

Daniel continued painting. "This wouldn't take long either if she were in here helping us."

"She'll be back soon."

It was clear Daniel was exhausted and irritated. She could tell by the way he made quick strokes with the brush instead of layering it on smoothly. How could she blame him? They'd started early that morning, just after sunrise, and the sun was dropping in the sky.

On top of that, she'd kept him from doing something he'd waited all winter to do—to fix up an old Schwinn bicycle that had belonged to his mother. He'd talked for years about bringing it back to life. It was against the back wall of the garage with flat tires. He just needed time to get it ready—for Lucy. He wanted to pass it down to her and teach her how to ride it that summer. She was standing in his way now, but she had no choice. They needed to get everything up and running at the parlor to get their lives back on track as soon as possible. They were almost finished anyway.

"I'm lucky you're here," she said in a soft voice.

He turned back and gave her a suspicious look. He softened a bit and then winked at her. "You're lucky I'm here too."

Nora laughed.

Lucy came out of the back hallway and stopped in front of her. "Mommy, Blanco's standing in the corner again."

"Doing what?"

"Nothing. Just standing there."

"He's just guarding the place," Nora said. "A real-life ghostbuster."

Lucy glanced around with wide eyes. "We have ghosts here?"

"Not anymore, sweetheart."

The cat came in a moment later and rushed over to Nora's feet. He circled her ankles and brushed against her pant leg. Only a few months earlier, she would have cringed at the cat's affection, maybe even pushed him away. Instead, Nora reached down and scratched the side of his neck for a moment before he rushed off again to Lucy's side.

"He loves you," Lucy said.

"I I—" She hesitated for a moment. Images of Blanco as he'd been months earlier still haunted the back of her mind, but she pushed them all away. Things were different now, in a good way. Her feelings toward Blanco had definitely changed a lot recently. "I love him too."

4

Nora had almost finished painting her side of the front room when the door to her father's old apartment at the back of the parlor clicked open. Ally entered a moment later. She was flipping through a book with her face down, and her hand obscured the title.

When Ally finally looked up, her face brightened as she glanced around at the walls. "Wow! Fresh paint makes a big difference."

"You're back," Nora said.

Daniel grumbled something and stepped down from his ladder, cleaning off his brush before dropping it into a pail of water. "I thought we agreed this would be a joint effort."

Ally swallowed. "I had some errands to run."

"So did I," he said.

"Sorry." She pushed her lips together.

Nora gestured to the book in her sister's hand, if only to interrupt Daniel. "Learning anything new?"

Ally looked down at it and nodded. "There are a lot of things I don't understand yet. I have to keep up with my research, you know, and since we're renovating the parlor, I thought now's a good time to invest in myself too. Professional development. I had better get all my terminology and facts straight before the clients come rushing through the doors. I haven't studied any of this since before my college days. It's like we're going back to basics."

The light in the room faded. The sun had passed behind some clouds outside. Daniel stepped to the front door and flipped on the lights for the first time that day. The colors looked somehow different under the parlor's dim lighting, not as vibrant as Nora had perceived only minutes earlier. The others didn't seem to notice. Daniel folded up the ladder, sealed the paint cans, and stepped down the hallway toward the bathroom.

At the same time, Lucy picked up Blanco and walked with him around the room in her arms, as if giving him a tour. She whispered into his face and cringed. "Do you like the new paint, Blanco? The colors are pretty, but it stinks, doesn't it?"

Just after Daniel stepped out of the room, Nora leaned into Ally to take advantage of the moment of privacy between them. She whispered, "How did it go at Father Tony's?"

"Just one box this time," she said.

"Anything interesting?"

"Just some books. Are you heading out?"

"Soon." Nora nodded. "Lucy's getting antsy."

Lucy stared at them from the corner of her eye and whispered again in Blanco's ear. "They're talking about us."

Ally laughed. "I can't get enough of that kid."

Lucy pretended not to hear, focusing on Blanco instead.

Ally walked over and brushed the back of Lucy's hair. "Hear that? I can't get enough of your precious little smile."

Lucy looked up now, glaring at Ally with narrowed eyes as if her aunt were teasing her. "I heard you."

"Do you need any help?" Ally glanced around the parlor. "Sorry I was late. It took me longer than I expected."

Nora shook her head. "We should be finished in a few days."

Ally nodded and folded her arms over her chest. "The place

looks great. I'm sure we'll get plenty of new clients. We may even need to hire some extra help."

"Hire someone?" Nora's eyes widened. "That's a scary thought. I never thought I'd consider taking it that far. Can we afford it?"

"I'll do the math." Ally glanced down at Lucy. "It might be cheaper than hiring a babysitter for Lucy over the summer after we're open for business. We've got to keep her distracted somehow."

"I'm not distracted," she said.

"I didn't mean it like that, goofball. You're amazing."

"I know." Lucy pulled Blanco in beside her and stroked his white fur, then turned to face Nora. "Can I sleep here with Aunt Ally tonight?"

Nora shook her head. "Not tonight."

Ally also shook her head. "I've got work to do."

"Aw." Lucy stroked Blanco's fur a little more, and he dropped over onto his side.

Ally moved in and kneeled down beside Blanco, stroking his fur just a bit above his chest. She pulled back suddenly and gasped. "Oh, my God."

"What happened?" Nora looked over at them crouched beside Blanco. Lucy was confused.

"Look." Ally set aside her book and shifted so Nora could see Blanco. Holding him still with one hand, she touched the side of his chest, drawing a line across the symbol that Gabriel had branded into him months earlier. The lines were darker than normal. Now blood red.

Nora rushed over. "Is he bleeding?"

"A trickle, maybe, but... it's not fresh. It's... hot."

"What do you mean, hot? Should we get him to the vet?"

"Mommy, what's wrong with Blanco?" Lucy looked scared, staring at Blanco with wide eyes.

"He'll be okay," Nora answered. "We'll have someone look at him. Don't worry."

Ally gently swept her fingers over the lines again. Blanco didn't seem to mind their attention. "Do you ever wonder what that means? The symbol?"

"I'd rather not think about Gabriel ever again—he's moved on... and so have I. The poor cat has suffered enough."

"I know," Ally said. "I just... wonder what he was thinking when he did such an awful thing."

Nora shook her head as if shaking the thought from her mind. "I'd rather not think about it. Gabriel wanted to take him with him, of course, to the other side. It's over now." She turned toward her daughter. "Lucy, get your things. We have to get you home now."

Ally stared at Blanco's copper eyes then took out her phone while Blanco was on his side, the symbol still facing her. Despite his thick white fur, the lines were clear. She took a few photos of it and then brushed his fur. When she set him down and backed away, Blanco ran into Lucy's arms.

"I wish that man hadn't done that to Blanco," Lucy said.

"I wish he hadn't done it either," Ally said. "But some people don't understand the pain they cause others."

"Can we please not talk about it anymore?" Nora cut in.

"Sorry." Ally met Nora's stern gaze and gave a sympathetic smile.

Her sister relaxed a moment later. "Forget it. Let's just focus on the bright future ahead for this place. Things will be different from now on."

"Yes, they will," Ally said.

"We'll never let anyone hurt you again," Lucy whispered into Blanco's face.

The cat purred.

Ally turned away and headed toward her apartment, zooming in on the photos she'd just taken. Over her shoulder, she spoke in a slower, distracted tone. "I'll be in Dad's apartment... I mean, *my* apartment."

$$\text{❧} \quad 5 \quad \text{❧}$$

Ally stepped into her father's old apartment and shut the door behind her. It didn't feel right to call it home yet—the place still smelled like her father's cheap cigarettes. She hadn't aired out the place enough. His presence was still there, along with all the faded childhood memories. Would the distinctive smells ever go away?

Moving toward the kitchen, she caught a glimpse of an open bedroom door—the room previously occupied by her parents. It was her room now, and the rooms where she and her sister had grown up were now a storage graveyard of everything her father had refused to let go. Outsiders would have considered them stuffed with piles of junk, but each item held a memory, good or bad. She'd barely made a dent in sorting through any of it, as she'd promised Nora she would.

At least the apartment was quiet and private. A perfect place to study without distractions, and she'd waited all day for this moment—to go through the items Father Tony had given her that morning, carrying them in through the back door before the parlor opened to avoid prying eyes.

All the blinds were closed, and she'd locked the door on the way in. The isolation made her heart race faster. This was her time to explore.

She stepped over to the kitchen table she'd cleared away for her research. She'd meticulously laid out Father Tony's gifts, with the researched items on one side and the new items on the other.

The mahogany box was there. She had unwrapped it as soon as she'd gotten home, but hadn't had time to finish her examination. When she touched its edges, Father Tony's voice echoed through her mind.

Promise me you'll dispose of this.

"I will," she reaffirmed while gazing down on it. "Right after I'm done with it."

She hadn't told Nora. Not yet. Her sister would insist on disposing of it just as Father Tony demanded. She wouldn't appreciate its true value. This was a key to something ancient, something *real*. And now she owned it.

Removing the crude loop of wire holding the rusted metal latch in place, she lifted the lid and peeked inside. The eyes of a statue greeted her—pierced her. But they weren't eyes. They were blackened, hollow eye sockets where the eyes should be. This thing wasn't human. Definitely not human. It had a human shape, but it was contorted, with its proportions all wrong. It more closely resembled a gargoyle, standing tall and filling the length of the box, with its wide mouth gaping to reveal rows of jagged teeth. Horns curled against its skull just above its ears. Its claws were jagged spikes protruding from twisted hands. It stood crooked and hunched forward as if it were moving in closer to whisper a secret.

She reached in without thinking about it, touched its cool surface, then lifted it out of the box. It was heavier than it looked and worn by time, with some parts blackened as if fire had touched it.

Her sister had never truly believed in the cult, had never believed in the practice they'd preached all their lives. But after standing in that circle with Gabriel and Anna a few months earlier, she'd felt a connection to something much darker in the universe, a bristling energy like the one she felt now after touching the statue. That same energy had almost killed them in Gabriel's house. But they had survived, and now she wanted more.

Laying the statue on its side beside her, she retrieved the next object from the box: a brittle parchment. She delicately unfurled it and scanned the obscure text.

What language was it? Latin? Hebrew? It would take more research to know the truth.

Beneath the parchment, someone had left behind a hand-drawn, crude sketch of a child. The small figure had large black eyes, and they were standing in front of a horned figure inside a circle of flames with their arms raised toward the creature.

Her heart pounded in her chest. The symbol in the sketch matched the one branded into Blanco's side: the symbol of Moloch.

She had to understand why Gabriel had crossed the line into such a dark world. What was the symbol? What was the symbol's meaning, its significance? And what was the significance of the items in the box that he'd left behind?

She tried to decipher a few of the words on the parchment, breaking down each one, letter by letter, although none of it seemed to fit together in her mind. The words meant nothing.

Her voice was barely a whisper as she tried to pronounce the first line of words. "Barash'ti... molakh... e'tzuh..."

The floor and wall made a cracking noise behind her, as though the foundation was settling. A chill swept up her spine, and she spun around.

No one was there.

Still, a heaviness settled into the room. Nothing physical, but an energy twisting through the air like invisible fingertips brushing over the back of her neck. Her mouth went dry.

Her ears perked within the silence, and her eyes narrowed.

Something was there. If only she could see beyond her reality. The temperature dropped. The light shifted as a silhouette appeared behind her blinds—the figure of someone peeking through the cracks. Someone was standing just outside her window.

Ally stumbled away from the table and called out, "Hello?"

Something pounded against her door and she shuddered. Then again. The sound echoed through her mind.

"Aunt Ally?" Lucy's small voice came from the other side. "Aunt Ally? Can I come in?" Another knock, but this time much softer.

Ally slipped the parchment and statue back into the box, and slammed the lid shut again before pushing it out of sight.

"Just a minute," she called out.

Lucy jiggled the door handle. "Aunt Ally?"

Ally rushed to the door and threw it open. Lucy stood trembling in the doorway with her arms crossed over her chest. The little girl's eyes were wide, and her face was pale.

Ally crouched down in front of her. "What's wrong?"

"Something hurt Mommy."

$$\text{\Large ❧ \quad 6 \quad ❧}$$

Nora was tired and ready to go home. Daniel was scrambling to wrangle Lucy as she chased Blanco from room to room. Her daughter was giggling, and judging from experience, it would take a coordinated effort to get her settled down. Nora smiled. It had been a good day. They'd gotten a lot done with the renovations, even without much help from Ally.

Her sister had vanished into the back apartment, leaving them to take care of things alone. It didn't matter so much, but they could have used the help. Nora let it go and grabbed Daniel's keys from the front desk.

"I'll pull the car around," she called out to him.

"We'll meet you out there," Daniel said from somewhere out of sight.

She stepped out of the parlor's side door to the small parking lot they shared with the other businesses next door. Daniel's SUV sat alone at the far end of the lot. Two lights illuminated the area: one just above the exit, attached to the side of the building, and the other a city light near the sidewalk in the other direction. She could see her way around well enough. It was a safe area of the city—safe enough—but she glanced in every direction as she walked toward the car.

The old building stretched out long, extending the full length of the parking lot. Her father's old apartment, where her family had grown up—now Ally's space—filled the back half. The light was on in the one barred window that faced the parking lot—a silhouette moved behind the blinds. No doubt Ally was reading or researching something.

Her sister had always been that way—a sort of recluse—hiding away from the world. Nora wanted to go back in there, throw down her book, and order her sister to get out there and take a risk for a change. *Anything* besides wasting another evening alone surrounded by books and silence. But it wouldn't have made any difference. Ally was always the stubborn one.

Nora pulled open the car door, and a rush of cold air swept in around her. She gasped, and the hairs at the back of her neck bristled.

Someone was approaching.

Not approaching. They were behind her.

She froze and then spun around.

Nothing.

Just an empty parking lot.

What the hell?

Just her nerves. It had been a long day. She needed sleep—maybe even a long bath and a little wine.

Another sound came from only a few feet away. It held a disturbing tone—like someone taunting her, insulting her. Words harsh and low. The sound reverberated through her body, almost moving her forward.

"Is someone there?" she called out.

No answer.

She stared across the car, and a chill swept down her spine. Was someone hunkered down back there, ready to pounce on her as soon as she came into view? She clutched her purse and keys, then backed away from the car. Her body tensed. She would run at the first sign of trouble.

Circling around the car, she found nobody hiding in the shadows. Nothing had moved. Nobody had jumped out at her or scrambled away.

Heading back to the driver's side door, something touched the back of her hand. It wasn't just the wind or her imagination. Something sharp had scratched across her skin. Slowly and intentionally.

She jerked her hand back, and the sensation faded.

Nerves? Insects?

It *was* that time of night when the bugs seemed to swarm beneath the lights. But it hadn't felt like an insect crawling.

Opening the car door again, she started to climb into the driver's seat.

This time, something shoved her forward. It came at her without a sound and hit her like a full-body slam from behind. Nora's shoulder hit the car with a sickening crack, and the air was knocked out of her lungs. She stumbled forward, struggling to stay upright as a trickle of air gradually flowed back in through her gaping mouth.

She didn't fall right away—not until the second blow came. Someone thrust her forward again. A crushing weight, like a massive fist, struck her back and tore away a piece of her jacket. The force overwhelmed her. Her knees buckled, and she collapsed to the ground.

The world moved in slow motion on the way down. Everything toppled sideways with no time to shield her face. Her forearm and shoulder bore the brunt of the impact. A burst of air filled her lungs at the same time.

When everything stopped, her forehead hovered an inch above the parking lot's asphalt. The tip of her nose rubbed against it.

What... just happened?

The weight on her back prevented her from turning around. If only she could get a look at her attacker's face...

They weren't making any threats—not a word—not even a single breath.

Scraping her chin against the coarse asphalt to turn her head, she glanced back from the corner of her eye. Nothing. Just shadows dancing at the edge of her vision.

I'm going to die.

The light above the parlor's side door exploded in a burst of sparks and then went dark. At the same time, the pressure against her back stopped.

Gasping for another breath, she braced herself for whatever was coming next.

Why is this happening?

But nothing came next. The weight on her back ended. It was gone, yet her head still reeled with pain. Cautiously, she rolled onto her side and glanced around the area.

She was alone.

Her car door sat open. Had they tried to steal her car or take something from it? Her aching body struggled to stand until fingers found the edge of the doorframe. She pulled herself up a little at a time, turning her gaze in every direction while taking in a full breath for the first time since being knocked down.

"Daniel," she cried out in a weak voice. "Ally."

No answer.

Staggering back inside the parlor through the side door, she slammed the door shut behind her. She found Daniel standing near the counter, halfway through switching off the lights. Lucy was curled in a chair with Blanco on her lap. The cat's ears shot up the second Nora slammed the door shut.

"Nora?" Daniel turned, smile fading as he saw her. His eyes went wide. "What happened?"

She struggled to answer. "Someone was there. Outside."

Lucy rushed toward her, her eyes full of concern and fear. "Mommy?"

"I'm okay," Nora lied. "It just... caught me off guard."

Daniel rushed to her side and wrapped his arm around her waist. "Your coat is torn. Did someone grab you?"

Nora shook her head. "They didn't take anything. Didn't say anything. Just... shoved me. Hard."

"I'm calling the police," Daniel said, pulling out his phone. "Did you see who it was?"

"No." Nora sank into one of the chairs in the front parlor. Her right wrist and shoulder throbbed. Maybe a bruise. Maybe broken. "It could've been anyone," she whispered.

Lucy ran to the back apartment. Nora could hear her daughter pounding on the door, and a short time later Ally rushed into the room, out of breath. "Oh, my God, Nora."

"Someone jumped me in the parking lot," Nora said. "I thought they were going to..."

Lucy approached Nora cautiously as if she might push her away. "Was it a monster?"

Nora shook her head. "No, sweetheart. Just a really bad person. I'm okay now," she lied. "Mommy's okay."

Ally swallowed. She was staring at Blanco. He'd moved near the window, staring out into the darkness with his tail flared. He let out a low snarl and then hissed into the night.

Daniel stayed on the phone with the 911 operator. Covering it for a moment with his palm, he said, "They won't be long. Can you describe him at all? Tall? Short? Fat?"

"No," Nora said. "It was too dark."

Ally gestured to something on Nora's jacket. Something dark smeared along her sleeve. Not blood.

Ash.

$\maltese$ 7 $\maltese$

After the police and paramedics had arrived, Nora had chosen not to go to the hospital. There were no serious injuries, just cuts and bruises. She hadn't felt it then, but whatever had torn her jacket had also left deep scratches down her back, drawing a bit of blood. Her muscles ached, but it was nothing she couldn't handle. It could have been a lot worse, they'd suggested.

The police had scoured the area and had found nothing. No sign of an assailant. Nothing to lead them to think that it was anything but an attempted carjacking or a sexual assault. She knew better. This wasn't random. This was an attack on *her*. Had she unwittingly pissed off another client? The confrontation with Gabriel months earlier still echoed through her mind. There were plenty of ghosts from her past that might come back to haunt her. Was this one of them?

She'd gone home after that, with the assault reverberating through her mind, but she kept quiet in the car. Ally had followed them home, even offering to stay the night if it would help, but Nora had insisted it wasn't necessary. Somehow, she knew the worst was over. At least for now.

Nora sat in the kitchen now, with her elbows on the table,

running her fingers through her hair. Daniel was doing the dishes, while Ally was putting Lucy to bed.

The routine should have comforted her. Daniel methodically working his way through the dishes stacked beside the sink, rinsing them and then putting them into the dishwasher. Everything was taken care of. Instead, the unease lingered at the back of her mind.

Ally stepped into the kitchen. Her tired eyes showed she was ready to go home. "I read Lucy a book. She's asleep... I think," she said softly, taking the seat across from Nora.

Nora looked up slowly. "Is she okay?"

Ally took a seat across from Nora and smiled warmly. "She was scared. But I told her you scared them away. I said you slipped, and they ran. She believed me."

Nora let out a short, humorless laugh. "I scared them off, huh? I must be more terrifying than I thought."

Ally's smile faded. "It made her feel better."

Daniel didn't turn around, but she could tell he was rattled by the attack, judging by the way he moved. He hadn't said much since they'd gotten home. But he didn't have to.

She stood and then immediately regretted it—her ribs ached. The scrapes on her back burned beneath the gauze. She steadied herself against the edge of the table.

"You should sit," Ally said gently. "You've been through a lot."

"I'm fine."

Ally frowned. "I know you don't believe that."

"It was just some nutcase trying to scare me, that's all."

A long silence stretched between them, and a nagging thought crept into her mind.

Who the hell attacked me?

They'd caught her off-guard, creeping up from behind, but why hadn't she managed to identify *something* about him? Their height, their weight, even their clothing. She hadn't seen any part of them clearly. It had all been a shadowy blur.

"You'll need to carry a weapon," Daniel said. "Pepper spray. Or a knife. Maybe even a gun."

"No guns," Nora said.

"You were violently assaulted tonight, Nora," Daniel said. "He shredded your coat. What do you think, that this was just a prank?"

"Of course not." Nora glanced at Daniel's back. He still hadn't turned around. "I'll get some pepper spray. It's not like I'm out looking for fights."

"Did he remind you of anyone?" Daniel asked.

"I'm not even sure it was a he."

"What about the smell?" Daniel glanced over his shoulder, watching her from the corner of his eye. "Did you smell anything? Like cigarettes or alcohol or cologne?"

"They didn't smell like anything."

"He must have made some noise—his footsteps during the struggle. Was he wearing sneakers or boots?"

"I don't know."

"Or maybe he let slip a word or whispered something?"

"Nothing." Nora shook her head again. "I know it's hard to believe something like this can happen without a clue."

Ally gave her a look of sympathy. "You're probably just still in shock. The trauma is clouding your memory. I'm sure something will come back to you in time."

"Maybe I don't want it to come back."

A sound drifted down from Lucy's room. They both looked toward the stairs at the same time.

Ally stood. "I'll check on her."

Once she disappeared around the corner, Daniel finally turned completely around, his face full of concern. "You're not fine."

Nora leaned forward and dropped her head into her hands. "Of course I'm not."

He wiped his hands on a towel and leaned against the counter. "I'm worried about you."

"I'll carry a weapon if you want," Nora said. "We can put up cameras."

"We have to do something. You were almost killed."

She met his gaze. "I wasn't almost killed."

He scoffed. "You need to take this seriously."

"I am taking this seriously."

"Then please stop acting like you're invincible."

"I never said—"

"You didn't have to."

"Listen... Can we just take a rain check on this conversation? I know what you're going to suggest—that I close the parlor and get a different career."

He didn't disagree. "Maybe it's time we reevaluate the situation."

She shook her head. "We've already had this conversation. What happened out there... It could have happened to anyone."

"You're not just anyone to me."

At least they weren't screaming at each other. There was restraint in his voice. Maybe because Lucy was sleeping. But maybe because they were both too tired to argue. If their past arguments were any guide, the tension would continue long into the next day, but she hated climbing into bed with him without a truce, without at least coming to some basic understanding between them.

She exhaled slowly. "What do you want me to do? I finally feel like I'm on the right path in my life. Ally is running the parlor now, and the renovations are almost done. I can't just hide away in a cave until all of this blows over."

"I want you to think of Lucy," he said. "It was bad enough that she saw you beaten up like that. What if you... hadn't come back?"

A wave of emotional pain swept through her. She pictured everything through Lucy's eyes just for a moment, and her own eyes watered. She'd said it so many times before, but she said it again, "This is my career, Daniel. It's all I know."

"I understand that," he said. "Let's just try to think a little more about what this is doing to her, even if you can't think of yourself or me. Maybe it will never happen again, but do we really want to take that chance? Some of the clients I've seen go in there… Some of them aren't… right, like that Gabriel guy."

She cringed at the memories of Gabriel that came flooding back. "Please don't bring him up again. He's dead. And I don't think the person who attacked me was one of my clients, anyway."

"How do you know?"

"I know."

"Still… I'm worried one of these times you'll end up in the hospital… or worse. Is that what you want?"

"Of course not," she said. "I'm sure it would never come to that."

"The bandages on your back tell a different story. What if this is just the beginning?"

She touched the bandages on her left wrist. "They just roughed me up a bit. That's all. Probably just a random attack, but I scared them away. It won't happen again."

"You don't know that. I know your priorities have shifted in the right direction after your father died, but please take things a little slower. Please? Lucy's scared. *I'm* scared." He stepped over and lifted her left hand, caressing her fingers and running his thumb over the bandage that covered her knuckles. "Show me you still care about us. I don't want anything to happen to you."

"I'm not going to leave the parlor," she said. "I can't. But I won't go out alone anymore, I promise. I'll bring Ally with me."

He stared at her and then kissed the top of her forehead. It was brief, but his face warmed her skin. He didn't back away for several seconds, hovering at the edge of embracing her, until Ally returned. He pulled away then and gently lowered her hand to the table without another word.

"She's asleep again," Ally said. "Just needed to sit with her for a minute."

Daniel quietly left the room.

Ally waited until his footsteps faded, then crossed to Nora. "Are you *really* okay?"

Nora shook her head. "I need help."

Ally raised an eyebrow. "The pepper spray kind?"

"Yes," Nora said, "but also... of a different sort."

Ally sat back down. "From whom?"

Nora looked past her, out the kitchen window into the thick darkness. "Father Tony."

❧   8   ❦

The next morning, Nora stood outside St. Michael's Catholic Church. She'd gotten as far as the door and then stopped. She hated stepping into a church—any church. There was just something about going through that door that churned her stomach. Her parents had taught her to distrust religions, but it wasn't just that. Maybe it was the way people glanced at her with a hint of judgment, or the sense that they were whispering about her behind her back. Still, she pushed aside her fears, took in a deep breath, and stepped inside.

The religious decor was overwhelming. It covered every surface. Light beamed through stained glass windows, and the vaulted ceiling in the sanctuary had a series of panels that showed the deeds of the saints and St. Mary.

She'd never been inside a Catholic church before, although she had attended Sunday services occasionally in nondenominational churches when she was a child. Her father had brought them there for "research," to show them how the "other half" lived, but also to help her give a more convincing performance in the parlor. It was always about the business.

An antique wood smell filled the air. Someone was singing a hymn behind closed doors to her left. A dozen parishioners sat scattered around the sanctuary, many of them kneeling near the front, peering up at the oversized crucifix with Jesus hanging on the cross above the altar. It loomed over the sinners below, lest they forget the evil they committed to the Savior two thousand years ago. There were some other parishioners huddled in the back with their heads bowed. Glancing around the room, Father Tony was not among them.

Before she could get too far, a man in a black suit approached her and asked, "May I help you?"

"I need to speak with Father de la Cruz," she said.

He smiled. "May I give him your name?"

She nodded and grinned. "Tell him Madame Lenora is here."

His eyebrows went up, and he studied her for a moment longer than necessary, then nodded and gestured toward a pew. "Wait here, please. I'll get him."

Nora took a seat on the nearest wooden bench. The sounds echoing through the sanctuary soothed her mind, but doubt crept in. Had she made the right choice in stopping by? Father Tony had helped them before, but how would he respond to her hands covered in bandages? She looked more frazzled now than ever before.

A moment later, the man in the black suit returned with Father Tony at his side. The father's bright expression warmed her heart. At least he seemed to remember her fondly. She mirrored his enthusiasm as he approached, greeting him halfway. She extended her arms, and they shared a brief but awkward hug, but his smile spread a little wider when they finally pulled away.

The man in the black suit walked away without another glance, leaving them alone.

"Nice to see you again, Nora," Father Tony said. "How may I help you?"

She glanced around. "Can we talk in private?"

He looked at her curiously. "Of course."

He led her down a narrow hallway stuffed with more religious decor before finally turning into what looked like an outer office.

A silver-haired woman sat behind a desk near the door. She studied Nora curiously for a moment, then turned to Father Tony. She opened her mouth as if to speak, but he silenced her with a small wave of his hand as he swept past her into his private office. Nora hurried to catch up to him, and he shut the door behind them once they were inside.

"The trick is to never stop," he said. "If my secretary gets a word in, we'll be standing there for an hour."

Nora chuckled.

"I'm afraid this is as private as it gets," he said.

His office was simple and organized. There were several framed pictures on one wall and a few framed diplomas on another. A pile of papers and a silver crucifix sat on his desk beside an open Bible in the center, marked with a red ribbon. She'd caught him working, maybe preparing for a sermon, and a pang of guilt swept through her.

"I hope I'm not bothering you," she said.

"No bother at all." He gestured to the chair in front of his desk. "I'm sure you wouldn't have come here unless it was important. So, please feel free to speak your mind. I know you've been through a lot lately."

Nora sat down. He didn't need to remind her of the night at Gabriel's house months earlier—the demon dogs and the fury in Gabriel's eyes. "We both have."

"That's true." He nodded solemnly. "How is your sister coming along with the items I gave her?"

"I saw she brought something into the parlor," Nora said. "She's like a child on Christmas morning."

"Not the sort of items I like to gift to anyone," he said, "but under the circumstances I believe Ally is the only one with enough knowledge or courage to handle such things. They're too dangerous to leave in the church or in my home."

Three tall windows loomed over his desk behind his chair. The one in the middle was made of stained glass and depicted Christ crucified on the cross.

She inched forward in her chair. How would she tell him about what had happened in the parking lot without sounding crazy? Of course, he would listen without judgment to anything she said, but even now she tried to rationalize it.

He gave a curious look and gestured to the bandages on her wrists. "I'm assuming you didn't come here to brighten an old priest's afternoon."

She smiled. "Not this time. Things have been... a little rough lately."

"I hope it's nothing serious." He straightened in his chair.

"No." She held up her hand with the bandages for him to see then turned it over and dropped it. "I survived."

"That doesn't sound good."

She leaned in a little closer. "Do you remember when we first met? When you came into my parlor after the birds broke through the front window?"

He grinned. "How could I forget?"

"Do you remember what you said? You warned me not to embrace the deception of my family's business, but you weren't condemning me. I know that now. You didn't try to publicly shame me or encourage me to shut down the parlor. Instead, you were only trying to shine a light on the dangers of my... profession."

He nodded. "I remember that."

"I've changed since then," she said. "I'm not the same person I was... even from a few months ago."

"We both have." He gave a small nod. "I share your sentiment. Seems we've both grown from our encounter at Gabriel's house."

"We're lucky to be alive." Nora glanced down. "But now... Now I feel... vulnerable."

"How so?"

"Last night," she said, "someone attacked me. I was walking to my car, and someone hit me from behind—knocking me to the pavement. They tore my jacket, I scraped up my hands, and

it knocked the wind out of me. Something—I don't know what...
who—held me on the ground, pressing something into my back
like a glove, a boot, or a fist. I was certain they were going to
kill me."

Father Tony stared at her solemnly. "I'm very sorry to hear
that, Nora. You didn't deserve that. Did you go to the police?"

"I did."

"Did they find the person?"

Nora shook her head slowly. "I couldn't give a description. I
didn't see anyone."

Father Tony gave a perplexed look. "What do you mean?"

"I'm not sure the person who attacked me was... alive."

His expression changed to one of sympathy. "The dead aren't
the only ones who answer when you knock on doors, Nora. You
may not want to rule out the living just yet."

"I wish I could believe that."

"Why not?"

"Because after they knocked me down—when I was gasping
for breath, and I thought they were going to finish me off—they
just stopped."

"They ran away," he said.

"No. They were just... gone. When I finally got the nerve to
look around, there was nothing. No one—not even footsteps."

His eyes widened. "Who do you think it was?"

"Not who—what."

He studied her for a long moment. "There are things I can't
explain, but we should be careful here to rule out all other
options before jumping to any supernatural conclusions."

"Nothing else makes sense. They didn't steal anything—
either from me or my car. Nobody tried to sexually assault me.
They just... disappeared."

"Have you done any séances recently?"

She shook her head. "Not since the incident with Gabriel. I
thought we'd left all of that behind."

"I believe you," he said. "It's just difficult to draw any conclusions based on what you're telling me. Anything is possible. But I can tell you this: evil isn't confined to haunted houses and remote cemeteries. It follows, it attaches, and sometimes, it tests the ones who have already stood against it."

She leaned forward. "What should I do?"

He leaned back and clasped his hands over his chest. When he finally opened his mouth to speak, someone knocked on the door. He glanced toward the sound. "Yes?"

"Father Tony?" the secretary's voice came from behind the closed door. "Your next appointment is here."

"Thank you," he said. "I'll just be a minute."

"Thank you," she said.

Turning his attention back to Nora, he peered into her eyes. "What would you like me to do? What feels right to you? I can stop by the parlor and bring holy water to bless the area, if that would help."

"Do you think it would?"

"It's hard to say. Of course, your experience is valid, and I'll help in any way I can."

The sounds coming from the outer office grew louder—the murmur of a man and the secretary talking. Father Tony seemed not to notice them, but she felt the pressure to say something.

She wanted to tell him she was certain her attacker wasn't something of this world. But that wasn't true. Doubt had crept in—the memory of the attack had blurred in her mind and faded over time. It could have been a man, although she didn't understand how that was possible. But how could she expect him to have answers when she couldn't even form the right question?

"Maybe I'm overreacting," she said. "It's possible, I guess someone—someone *real*—attacked me."

He looked at her for a long moment. "Are you sure?"

"No," she said, "but it was dark. Everything was dark. Maybe I... should just—"

He glanced over his desk, then lifted an oversized metal

crucifix from a worn cloth and extended it toward her. "Please take this."

She accepted it. Its weight startled her, heavier than she'd thought, but only about six inches high, and the metal chilled her palm.

"Thank you," she said. "What should I *do* with it?"

"Keep it with you," he said. "Keep it close. Whether your experience resulted from the living or the dead is irrelevant. Evil is evil, and you should take steps to protect yourself on all sides. Given your background, it's better to take every threat seriously."

The conversation in the outer office grew louder behind them.

Father Tony cleared his throat. "If you remember anything else about the attack, or if you'd like me to stop by or just want to talk, please don't hesitate to contact me. My prayers are with you."

She could tell by the weight in his voice that he wasn't just trying to soothe her—he meant it. She stood gripping the crucifix against her chest. "Thank you."

"May God bless you and keep you safe."

$$\text{❧}\quad 9 \quad \text{❧}$$

Ally held the ladder for Daniel. He was near the top, stretching to remove an old lighting fixture on the ceiling. The new one was on the floor beside Ally, still in its plastic wrapping. It was perfect—black iron and three amber glass globes. She had picked it out herself at the antique store down the road —something to give their newly renovated parlor a touch of class, in her opinion. Something her father had never bothered to pursue in all the years they'd lived there.

Daniel had cut the electricity, and the room was quiet except for the muffled drone of traffic outside and Lucy's humming as she sat cross-legged on a rug in the corner. Blanco was with her, sprawled on the floor beside her. His tail twitched every few seconds. They were both watching Daniel install the light with great interest. Lucy broke from humming every once in a while to whisper something, maybe some reassuring words directed at Blanco.

"Can you hand me the mounting bracket?" Daniel called down.

Ally passed it up to him. "Here you go."

He took it with a brief nod and started screwing it into place.

Almost in a panic, Lucy jumped to her feet. Blanco had raced across the floor, passing under the ladder on his way toward the back of the parlor. Lucy scrambled after him, knocking her shoe against one of the legs of the ladder.

Daniel cursed under his breath, shook his head, and continued. "Ally, please do me a favor. Take her back to the apartment. I'm afraid someone's going to get hurt."

Ally didn't let go of the ladder. It wasn't wobbling, but he was near the limits of his reach. "Will you be all right?"

"Sure," he said. "I've got the wiring ready. I just need to place it up there and connect everything."

Ally nodded, although he'd already turned his attention back to the ceiling.

Lucy disappeared down the back hallway to the apartment and returned a moment later. "Aunt Ally? Blanco wants to go into your house."

"How do you know?" Ally asked.

"He's scratching at the door."

"That's weird." Ally followed Lucy through the hallway to the back and found Blanco pacing back and forth in front of the door. He turned back when they approached, then he started scratching at the door again and stood on his hind legs while clawing at the wood. Ally stepped over and nudged in beside him.

"I think he's hungry," Lucy said.

"You fed him at home this morning, right?"

"Yes," she said. "He's hungry again."

Lucy yanked at Blanco, trying to move him out of the way, but he resisted. As soon as Ally opened the door a few inches, Blanco pushed his way through the opening and rushed inside.

"Maybe you're right," Ally said.

She had a little cat food but not much. It didn't seem to matter though after Blanco raced toward the kitchen and jumped onto the table using a chair along the way. He disappeared behind the box she'd retrieved from Gabriel's house.

Lucy ran to him, pushing the box out of the way to reveal

Blanco perched on the wooden box she'd opened earlier. He was staring at her with a smug grin. Lucy grabbed him with both hands and lifted. He let out a loud hiss while showing his teeth.

Lucy lurched back with wide eyes. "Bad kitty!"

Tension rose between them. Blanco repositioned himself on his wooden box throne but didn't back down. His chest came into view. Ally leaned in to get a better look, and he allowed her to push back his fur a bit. The scars lining his underside were inflamed again—thick and red.

"He's acting weird," Lucy said.

"Yes, he sure is." Ally watched him for a few seconds. Father Tony *had* warned her to keep Blanco away from it. "There's something going on with his scars—something's irritating them. He's probably in a little pain, so maybe be careful when you hold him. I think your mom still has some of the medicine the vet gave him from the last visit. Give him some of that as soon as you get home. The only thing we can do now is to keep him comfortable."

Lucy cautiously stroked his fur. Blanco allowed the affection but didn't budge.

"What's he sitting on?" Lucy asked.

Ally wasn't sure how to answer. Instead, she reached under Blanco, gripped the box with both hands, and tipped it sideways until he surrendered, stepping off it with another hiss. As soon as it was free, she pulled away the box. "Sorry, little guy."

Lucy's eyes lit up as she stared at the symbols etched into the box's cover. "What is it?"

"It's..." Ally considered explaining it with a lie. There were all sorts of options—something she'd found, something she'd bought, a gift from a friend. But Lucy deserved the truth. She had grown up surrounded by all things occult, like Ally and Nora had, so it was better to just get it out in the open, talk about the strange, twisted, scary things she encountered every day. Better to deal with it now than in a therapy session years from now. "It belonged to Blanco's former owner. Someone gave it to me to study."

Lucy fixated on it for a little too long. "What's in it?"

"Just some old stuff."

Blanco refused to leave the table, watching them with an icy stare while his red scars throbbed. Lucy leaned toward him with a stern face, but she didn't touch him this time.

"Blanco," Lucy said. "You shouldn't be on the table."

"He's okay," Ally said, "for now."

Lucy turned her gaze back to the box. "Where did it come from?"

"That's a good question," Ally confessed. "That's what I'm trying to figure out. It's connected with the occult, so I doubt your mom would approve of me showing it to you. She's trying to get rid of stuff like this—erase everything our parents taught us."

"Why?"

"She's scared, I think."

"Scared of what?"

Ally stared into Lucy's eyes. "That you'll get hurt."

Lucy didn't flinch. "I'm not afraid."

"I know," Ally said. "I know you're not, but we still need to always be careful. Do you remember what your grandfather talked to you about in here while he was alive?"

She nodded. "About séances and how to talk to dead people."

"Did that scare you?"

She shrugged. "A little. It sounded like stories."

"Some of it *is* stories." Ally stepped over and wrapped her arm around Lucy's back. "But some of it is real and a little scary at first, but after you learn, after you understand what it's all about, then you won't be afraid. Our family business was built on facing stuff like this. Your grandparents learned about it from their parents, and their parents learned about it from the ones before them.... It's in your blood."

Lucy looked at one of her arms.

"Not really *in your blood*," Ally clarified. "I mean, it's a part of your family history, passed down through generations. What I'm trying to say is, it's better for you to know the truth. Most people are afraid because they don't understand what they're seeing, so it's better to face your fears early because you'll see a lot of scary things in your life. There's a science to it, if you know what to study."

Lucy was staring at her with wide eyes. "Do you mean about all the ghosts?"

"Yes," she said. "There are ghosts out there."

Lucy glanced around the room. "What about in here?"

Ally hesitated to answer. Fear had spread over Lucy's face. "I wouldn't worry about ghosts. They won't hurt you. But that's what your grandparents did all their lives—although none of it was real. They were just performing."

"Tricking people," Lucy said.

Ally nodded once. "Yes. That's what we used to do, but now we're not tricking them anymore. We're only going to do what's real from now on. We want to educate people, help them not to be afraid."

"I like that." Lucy nodded, but her gaze jumped back to the table. "Can I see what's in the box? I think Blanco knows."

They both glanced back at Blanco. He was staring at the box.

"I think he might," Ally said.

She turned the box toward her and lifted the lid. The parchment lay in the same spot, but she didn't unscroll it this time—it was far too brittle to casually open for an eight-year-old. "It's a very old document. I'll probably need to get someone to translate it."

Lucy reached out and touched it.

Blanco growled this time. Not at Lucy or Ally, but at the open box.

Ally started to shut the lid but stopped. The parchment sat on a black cloth, but something poked out from under the edge. Another document? She lifted the parchment and removed a folded note with someone's name written in a feminine script across the front. *For Gabriel.*

The paper contained a list of handwritten instructions, steps for how to do some kind of ritual. There was a name and an address at the bottom, except that was written in someone else's handwriting. Gabriel's? It read: *Tess. 2112 Sawyer Way.*

"What's that?" Lucy asked, craning her neck around to look over Ally's shoulder.

Ally angled the page away from her but gestured to the instructions. This wasn't something for a child's eyes—it included steps on branding a symbol into flesh. It wasn't particularly graphic—reading more like a technical manual—but it detailed the steps to apply the brand precisely, how to shape the branding iron out of a piece of sculpted wire, and how to keep the animal bound and positioned properly. This is what Gabriel had used to brand Blanco.

Her stomach churned, but Lucy was waiting for an answer. "People sometimes perform rituals to connect with dark energy. Sometimes they do awful things."

"Why?" Lucy asked.

"Usually to get something in return, or at least that's the theory behind it."

Lucy caught sight of a symbol near the bottom of the page, and she pointed to it with a bit of glee. "That's the symbol on Blanco!"

"Yes," Ally said. "That's the one."

"What does it mean?"

"It's an occult symbol," she said, leaving out any mention of demons or animal mutilations.

"So, Blanco is evil?"

Ally met Lucy's gaze and shook her head. "No," she said. "Not at all. Although his former owner might have tried to make him that way."

Lucy tried to embrace Blanco, moving her face toward his fur, but he pulled away, jumping in front of the box again and letting out another hiss. The scars on his chest were almost bleeding as he sat staring at Ally.

Ally folded the paper and stuffed it into the box again before closing the lid. The name on the paper reverberated through her mind—Tess. A friend of Gabriel's?

"Tess," she said out loud by accident, almost in a whisper, but Lucy had caught it.

"Who's Tess?" she asked in her little voice.

Ally shrugged. "I'm not sure. Listen, your mom will be here soon, and this might be a little too much for an eight-year-old. Sorry if any of it scares you."

"I said I'm not scared."

Lucy held a stoic stare—a distinctive look Nora sometimes exhibited—but the innocence behind her eyes betrayed her youthful vulnerability.

"Okay." Ally leaned back. "We'd better get back out into the parlor. Your mom will be here soon, and I should probably check on your dad. We don't want him to get hurt, do we?"

"No."

"We'll continue our discussion another time, okay? Maybe when you're a little older, you'll understand it better."

"I'm not dumb," she said.

Ally turned to face her directly. "No, you're not. Sorry, I didn't mean it that way. But this... It's a lot to process."

Lucy shrugged and glanced at Blanco. "Get off the table, Blanco. Get down."

He still didn't budge, even after Ally put away the box, hiding it in a storage closet near the door. But after they shut off the lights, stepped out into the hallway, and glanced back at him sitting alone on the table in the darkness, he lurched forward and ran to join them.

Ally locked the door behind them.

Nora came into the parlor soon after they did. She seemed a bit dazed.

Daniel had completed the installation of the new ceiling

lamp. He was folding up the ladder as they moved their conversation behind the parlor's front desk.

"Are you okay?" Ally asked. "Did everything go okay with Father Tony?"

Nora nodded slowly while stepping around to the back of the front counter and removing her jacket. "He had plenty to say, but…"

"You didn't get the answer you wanted," Ally said.

She shook her head and then seemed to snap out of her daze. She turned toward Lucy, who was watching them from the hallway.

"Hi, Mommy," she said with a bright smile.

Nora extended her arms, and Lucy rushed to embrace her mother. "Hi, sweetheart, did you have fun this morning with Aunt Ally?"

Lucy looked at Ally with the hint of a devious grin mixed in with her smile before turning back to her mother. "I always have fun with her."

"Perfect," Nora said. "We have to open soon, so please take Blanco into the back and play. Can you do that?"

"Of course!" She didn't say anything about Blanco's inflamed scar or the box or Tess to anyone. Instead, she just nodded and ran off to one of the rooms at the back of the parlor.

As they prepared for the first customer, Ally couldn't get the name out of her mind.

Tess.

Father Tony might know who it was, but there was no need to bother him with it. She had the address. After everyone went home that evening, she could go there herself and bring the box. It wouldn't hurt just to stop by.

❧ 10 ❧

Nora was exhausted after a long day's work. She was on her way out the door with Lucy by her side when Ally stepped over to her, holding out something wrapped in a cloth.

"What's that?" Nora asked.

"Take it," Ally said, nudging the cloth toward her. "Just in case."

Nora recognized the shape—their father's Smith & Wesson 9mm handgun, in its case—and she gasped while her heart beat faster. She met Ally's gaze. There was worry on her sister's face. They had talked about getting her some pepper spray to protect herself, but not even for a moment had she considered going to this extreme.

"I'm not—" Nora said.

"Just take it." Ally pushed it closer.

She nodded and accepted it, turning away from Lucy quickly and slipping the handgun into her purse. When she turned back, Lucy had dropped beside Blanco's carrier, poking her fingers in at him playfully. He didn't seem amused.

"Time to head out, kiddo," Ally said, walking toward Lucy and gesturing for her to stand.

Lucy jumped up, then lifted the carrier with a bit of a struggle until Nora stepped over and took it away from her.

"Careful not to drop him," Nora said. "He wouldn't like that."

"I would never drop him. Not in a million years."

Ally walked beside them until they stepped outside through the side door. She gestured to Nora's purse. "Don't be afraid..."

"I won't."

She knew what her sister meant. *Don't be afraid to use it.* But Nora had no intention of ever digging it out, much less firing it at someone. Still, she *did* feel better.

Nora took Lucy's hand before heading out across the parking lot. She only made it a few steps before the anxiety surged through her chest. The attack had obviously affected her more than she'd imagined.

It was getting dark, and Daniel hadn't fixed the broken light yet. The streetlight provided some illumination, but not much. It was enough to light the way, but just dark enough to mess with her imagination.

Her car was near the back, beside Ally's car. The only two cars in the parking lot. But the pine trees and shrubs that lined the edge of the lot held plenty of shadows, and every shadow seemed to shift when she focused on it.

As soon as she reached her car, she loaded Blanco's carrier into the backseat. Lucy jumped into her own car seat and buckled herself in.

Nora glanced back one last time before climbing into the driver's seat. Ally was still watching from the doorway. She waved, and Nora nodded.

Dropping her purse on the passenger seat, she sensed the pistol's added weight.

Was it really necessary?

I hope I never find out.

She locked the door too. Just in case.

Overly cautious?

Maybe. But it helped.

She took a deep breath and then headed back out onto the main street. Her skin itched beneath the bandages. She wanted to rip them off, but they were necessary and would probably irritate her for another week—at least. A constant reminder of her vulnerability.

The car was quiet on the way home until Lucy broke the silence.

"I love Aunt Ally," her little voice came from the back seat.

Nora glanced at her in the rearview mirror with a warm smile. "I love her too. What did you do while I was gone?"

"We talked."

"About what?"

Lucy hesitated. "We talked about how knowing things is sometimes scary."

Nora's smile faded. "Yes. Unfortunately, that's right."

"Mommy," Lucy said.

"Yes?"

"Can we *really* talk to dead people?"

Nora hesitated before she answered. "We *can*, but... Why?"

"Aunt Ally said we can."

"Is that scary to you?"

"No."

"Good," Nora said. "Do you miss someone? Grandma or Grandpa?"

"A little," she said, "but I don't want to talk to them anymore."

"Why not?"

Lucy scoffed. "Because they're *ghosts*, Mommy."

Nora laughed. "I don't blame you, but sometimes people feel the need to say goodbye to their loved ones after they've passed on. They have a hard time letting go. That's just part of the grieving process, and I don't blame anyone for feeling that way."

"So ghosts are real, right?"

Nora hesitated to answer. She wanted Lucy to believe, but also to question everything. "Yes, but they're not *all* real."

Lucy nodded slowly. "So how do I know which ones are real?"

"You'll know," she said. "But be skeptical—question everything. There are genuine mediums out there, like your Aunt Ally, but there are a lot of fake ones too."

"I know she's real," Lucy said.

"Yes, maybe the last true medium out there."

After a while, Nora glanced back at Lucy. She was staring out the window. Her daughter had "wise" eyes, something Nora's father also had, although he'd never used his wisdom for anything good in his life. Not a single thing. Still, her heart ached at the thought that he was gone.

"Your grandpa would be so proud of you," Nora whispered.

Lucy met her gaze in the rearview mirror and smiled.

A shadow flashed in front of her car.

Nora slammed her foot on the brakes and screamed. She jerked the steering wheel sideways without thinking. A few seconds later, she straightened the car, but her heart was pounding.

Something had passed in front of her headlights. A bird, a dog, or maybe just a shadow? Definitely not her imagination. Shadows didn't move like that.

It had stood on two legs, but hunched forward like a disfigured coyote—its arms were too long, and its torso stretched too tall.

An animal? It wasn't human, at least. But it had *stood* like a man.

A black bear?

Too gaunt to be a bear. And no fur. Skin like burnt leather.

Its face.

She had seen its face and eyes for a moment, but that was enough. Its wide black eyes had reflected no light, and its gaping mouth held rows of rotting teeth. It had stood like a man, but it wasn't human. Nothing about it was human.

Or natural.

Her heart was pounding again.

"Was that a ghost, Mommy?" Lucy asked.

Nora swallowed and forced herself to take a deep breath before answering. "No. Definitely not."

❧   I I   ❧

As soon as Ally stepped onto the woman's porch, the light came on although she hadn't heard any motion sensor click. A moment later, the front door opened, and an unassuming woman appeared in the doorway. She was tall and elegant in a theatrical sort of way, with brown hair swept back, streaked with a bit of gray. She was dressed in a modest lavender sweatshirt and slacks.

Her sharp eyes scanned Ally for a moment, then stopped on the box in Ally's hand, and her brows jumped. "Well, that's something I never thought I'd see again."

"Are you... Tess?" Ally asked.

"Professor Caldwell. Tess. I'm sorry—have we met before?"

Ally opened her mouth to answer then glanced down at the box in her hand. "I—"

"Where did you find it?" Tess asked. "Oh. It doesn't matter." The woman pushed the door open wider and gestured forward. "Please come inside... before the bugs do."

Ally followed the woman inside, and the door clicked shut behind them. "I'm sorry to bother you."

"Not a bother," the woman said. "Not at all."

Without saying another word, Tess led her beyond the entryway. They passed a small office lined with shelves full of books, framed pictures, and antiques. One of the photos caught Ally's eye. A woman, a man, and a young girl stood barefoot in the sand with the ocean's waves crashing behind them. The woman was Tess, no doubt, with her arms stretched wide beside the man, and the child beaming up at both of them, her tangled hair twisting in the wind.

There was music playing softly in the background, coming from somewhere near the living room. It was a soothing classical number, although Ally didn't recognize it.

Tess glanced back at the box in Ally's arms as they continued forward. "Are you returning it to me?"

Ally looked down but didn't offer to share it yet. "I was hoping you could tell me a few things about it."

Tess led Ally toward the dining room. "I can tell you more than a few things about it. I'm a professor of anthropology at the University."

Ally swallowed.

They passed an antique hutch stuffed with pottery, photos, woven baskets, necklaces, and a row of figurines. No doubt, antiques she'd collected from around the world in her anthropology pursuits.

Stopping beside the dining table, Tess turned back to face her. "I don't get many visitors these days. You're braver than most to walk up that steep hill."

"It's... a nice walk. And it's nice to get out of the city once in a while. This is a quiet area."

Tess nodded. "Quiet can be a good thing... or it can mean there's no one left to talk to. I'm sorry, I didn't get your name."

"Ally," she said. "Ally Vale from The House of Vale. We own a psychic parlor in Minneapolis."

The woman's eyes widened. "Oh, I... I didn't recognize you." Tess seemed to study her face. "You do have your mother's eyes."

"You knew my mom?"

"I knew her well. We attended college together... until she

dropped out early. She was a few years younger than I, and we pursued different degrees, but our shared interests brought us together. It's funny that we became friends. As a child, my parents used to take me into that very same parlor every Sunday afternoon for a reading. They were believers—firm believers—in all things not-of-this-world. Your grandparents used to give me palm readings, predict my future—things of that type. My parents thought I had psychic abilities and pressured me to develop them. God knows I tried, but I just didn't have the gift, I guess."

"Sounds like we had similar experiences," Ally said.

Tess looked at her intently with a hint of a grin. "Do you have the gift?"

Ally gave a brief nod. "I've always been in tune with that stuff —probably the only one in my family. My parents always wanted my sister to take over the family business, but she never had a passion for it. After my father died recently, she was glad to finally step away, at least from her prior role. I took over the business, but her family still helps."

"And your mother, Claire? Is she still practicing?"

At the sound of her mother's name, Ally's chest tightened. She glanced down. "She passed away a few years ago."

Tess's shoulders slumped, and she frowned sympathetically. "That's tragic. So young. We shared so many wonderful times together at the University, until she dropped out to focus on her career at the parlor. A young man came along and stole her heart. I believe his name was Frank?"

Ally frowned. "That's my father. I don't think Mom voluntarily dropped out. Dad pressured her."

"That's a shame. We loved all the same things back then. She was a wonderful person. We were friends—on a certain level. How is your father these days?"

"He passed away a few months ago. Heart attack."

Tess's expression softened. "Oh, I'm very sorry to hear that. You've seen a lot of heartache lately."

"It's been... difficult, but we've recovered... mostly."

"I'm sure." Tess nodded sympathetically.

Ally met the woman's warm gaze. "You knew my father too?"

Tess shook her head. "I never met him. And unfortunately, after Claire dropped out of college, we grew apart. But it's all for the best, right? They were happily married, from what I heard —" Tess gestured toward Ally. "—and had a lovely daughter."

"Two daughters," Ally said. "I have a sister."

"I'm sure your parents loved each other very much." Tess studied Ally's face for a moment. "So you're the last medium in your family?"

"It seems so."

"Forgive me, but what's your sister's name?"

"Nora. Her parlor name is Madame Lenora."

"Yes, that sounds familiar." Tess nodded. "Well, whether or not your parents were truly psychic, I'm not sure. It didn't seem to make any difference. My parents were killed in a car wreck when I was fifteen, and they sent me to live with my grandparents in this very house. They took care of me, and I took care of them until they passed away several years ago. My career in anthropology kept me busy until recently. Lately, life's been a struggle, to put it mildly. It was a monumental task to manage everything alone near the end of their lives, along with caring for my daughter. I'm divorced. My husband... well, he found someone more *compatible*. But my daughter and I survived, and with any luck, things will improve."

Ally glanced around the room. There were no signs of anyone else in the house.

"Eve is a bit shy." Tess cleared her throat and shook her head with a little smile. "Oh, this is getting far too heavy for our first conversation, isn't it, dear? Tell me, how is your business doing?"

"We're renovating the parlor right now. I live in the back, where we grew up, and I guess I run the place now, although my sister's husband is taking care of most of the renovations. Lucy helps too."

"Lucy?"

"Their daughter," Ally said. "She's only eight, but she keeps things... lively."

"A child of that age is a handful, I know." Tess met Ally's gaze. "Does she have the gift too?"

Ally thought about it for a moment. "I'm not sure, but I guess time will tell. She *seems* to be interested in our family's history."

Tess pulled out a chair at the table and then gestured to a seat across from her. "Please. Have a seat." She pushed aside a decorative arrangement of items at the center of the table—a wide wooden bowl filled with leaves, stones, seashells, and pale objects, along with an ivory-handled knife, half-hidden beneath the clutter.

Ally sat across from the woman and placed the box on the table between them.

"The box." Tess let out a breath, studied her for a moment, before turning her gaze to the box between them and gesturing to it. "May I ask where you found it?"

"Does it belong to you?"

"A box like that doesn't belong to anyone. I possessed it for a time."

"It came from the home of Gabriel Flores," Ally said. "Did you know him?"

Tess's expression changed as if a painful image had flashed through her mind. "He was a client... for a time. Despite my lack of psychic abilities, I also make a little extra money on the side dealing in rare antiquities, specializing in the occult. I met him quite unexpectedly. He approached me after I'd finished giving a lecture at the University on ancient cultures, and wanted to know if it was possible to contact the dead. Of course, my expertise revolves around ancient artifacts, but I'm sometimes hired to handle more difficult cases of a personal nature. I like to help others... when I'm asked. Was he a friend of yours?"

Ally shook her head. "He was our client too, for a time."

"I see."

"We received it through a friend of his."

"What friend? May I ask?"

"A neighbor," Ally said.

Tess nodded and leaned back. "Gabriel purchased it from me."

"There was a parchment inside," Ally said, "along with a statue."

"The parchment and the statue go together."

"And also a handwritten note... from you."

"My instructions," she said. "Gabriel needed help to accomplish his goals."

"What goals?" Ally asked.

"If he was your client, then I'm sure you already know—to speak with his daughter one last time, to find closure. I tried to help him, but he didn't listen."

The sound of wheels moving across hardwood floors came from somewhere down the hall.

"Mama?" a girl's voice said. "The door is stuck again."

Tess glanced back. "I'll be right there, honey."

A teenage girl in a wheelchair came through the doorway and stopped. It was the same girl from the pictures in the office. With wide eyes, she stared at Ally nervously.

Turning back to Ally, Tess gestured with her head toward the girl. "This is my shy little shadow, my daughter, Eve."

Ally smiled at her, but the girl's expression didn't change.

"It's okay, Eve," Tess said. "This is Ally. We're just having a conversation."

"Hello." Ally widened her smile and gave a little wave.

Still no response.

"Eve," Tess said. "Come over and meet our guest."

Eve rolled forward into full view and forced a smile, although she still didn't say anything.

"My daughter is my *life*. A crash paralyzed the poor dear when she was fourteen by a drunk driver. It almost took her life.

The doctor said she would never walk again, but I still hold out hope for a treatment someday. The medical system abandoned her, as they do so many others."

"I'm sorry to hear that."

Tess's gaze jumped to the box again. "What do you plan to do with it?"

Ally ran her fingers along the edges. "I'm not sure. I'd like to know first how this was supposed to help Gabriel."

Tess sat back in her chair while Eve waited silently a few yards away. "I provided it to him for protection."

"Protection?" Ally asked. "The statue inside. It looks demonic."

Tess didn't look away. "The statue holds no danger. It's a safeguard, a vessel, but not one that summons anything on its own. It's more like a lock, a spiritual lock. The parchment and the instructions I gave to Gabriel don't summon anything. They just fortify the doors."

"You mentioned Moloch in your note," she said. "Isn't Moloch a demon?"

"He *is* a demon," Tess said, "but that doesn't mean he's being summoned by the statue. The first ritual, the one I provided to Gabriel, doesn't do anything more than use his domain as a shield. The statue is of Ezeran, a helper demon."

Ally furrowed her brow. "I've never heard of him."

"It provides a powerful barrier against lesser spirits from intruding. That's all it is."

"The statue looks old," Ally said. "Do you know where it came from?"

"It's hard to say," Tess said. "I discovered it in a local quarry when I was in college. Who can say when it was created? Or for what purpose?"

Ally opened the box and stared down at the parchment. "I went through the process on my own before I knew any of this. I'm afraid I released something."

Tess grinned. "If you followed the instructions in the box, the only thing you released is protection."

"No evil spirits or dark energy?"

"Of course not," Tess said with a small laugh. "Ezeran's statue is a tool for many things—transforming pain, gaining wealth, and of course, personal growth. He's associated with Moloch, yes, but if used correctly, the potential is unlimited."

"But Gabriel—he used this to evoke something dark, didn't he? He killed his dogs and branded them with a fire poker."

Tess winced. "He didn't follow my instructions. He rushed through it and let his emotions get in the way. Tragically, he took things much too far, judging by the information I read online about the incident. I tend to notice news of that type, when it happens."

Ally glanced down at the box. Looking up again, she met Tess's gaze. "I think Gabriel caused my father's heart attack, to some degree."

Confusion spread over the woman's face. "In what way?"

The memories of Gabriel's first visit to the parlor came flooding back. "He came into the parlor asking for our help. He wanted to contact his deceased daughter, like any other client, but we didn't provide an authentic séance—we never did. That's just the way things were back then when my father ran the place. Anyway, things went wrong, and Gabriel discovered our fraud. He stormed out of the place, furious—rightfully so."

Tess leaned back in her chair. "I see."

"That's not all," Ally continued. "He returned—his spirit did —shortly after he died and started terrorizing the parlor and my sister's family. When my father had a heart attack, he wasn't himself. It was Gabriel speaking through him, I'm sure. His last words were, 'How does it feel, Nora?'. Gabriel blamed my sister for everything that went wrong near the end of his life, and he took it all out on her by taking my father's life. I saw his suicide note. He wanted to destroy her."

Tess stared silently for a moment before her posture wilted.

"That's truly heartbreaking. It was never my intention to cause anyone any harm. The help I provided to Gabriel... I never expected anything like this to happen. He abused my trust."

Ally nodded slowly. She ran her fingertips over the top of the box, following the grooves and the worn texture. "His spirit is gone now—we helped him move on—but something else is still there."

"How do you know?"

"I know."

Tess stared into her eyes. "Yes, I suppose you do."

An image of her sister recovering after the attack flashed through Ally's mind. "Gabriel's spirit was behind my father's death. This time, it's not him. Something else is at work. Something worse."

"You believe you're in danger?"

"Not me," Ally said. "Nora's family. Something is there. I can feel it."

Tess's face was full of resolve. "Yes... and I can help you. This is all my fault, but I can make this right for you."

"How?" Ally asked.

Tess glanced down at the box. "You hold the answer in front of you."

"The box?"

Tess nodded. "Protection from the evil forces. It will work. Once someone performs the ritual in your sister's house, no dark entities will be able to touch them."

Ally stared at the cryptic patterns etched into the surface of the box. The lines and curves fascinated her. They were beautiful, but they also unsettled her in a strange way. "That's all I need to do?"

"That's all. One simple rite. No invocations. Just follow the instructions exactly as written. After it's done, nothing can enter that space unless it's invited."

"So, what did Gabriel do wrong?" she asked.

Tess's expression tightened. "I assume you're familiar with at least some of the details, since you have the box. He demanded a full manifestation of his daughter—not just her voice, but to see her again. That's not what the protection rite was intended for. He tried to force his will into existence through manipulation and the wrong words. The boundary protecting him collapsed."

"So, if I step through only what I see in the box, that's completely safe, right?"

"Yes," she said. "This part is safe."

"So, there are other parts to this ritual?"

She nodded slowly. "There are, but I refuse to provide them... to anyone. This ritual—the one in the box—is the outer ring, like a circle of salt."

"But I've read that the demon Moloch demands a child sacrifice for his help."

Tess nodded solemnly. "That's correct *if* you follow through with all the steps, which I refuse to provide. Gabriel crossed the line and offered his children in exchange for safe passage to see Anna."

"But he only had one child, Anna, didn't he?"

Tess shook her head. "His dogs were also his children, in a sense, and they were enough—or so he thought. Rituals like this are useful to some and abused by others. There's nothing inherently dangerous about them if you know how to use them properly. Follow the steps on the note in the box, read from the parchment as I instruct, and keep the statue in the home of the one needing protection."

Ally leaned back. It sounded so simple. A rising realization buzzed in her chest. *She* could do this. "And that's it?"

"Yes. Do this, and your sister's family will be protected from malicious spirits, assuming there are any nearby."

A rush of fresh energy surged through Ally. This was a way to finally connect with a power greater than herself, to finally put into practice everything she'd learned over the years. This was something *real*.

She nodded—maybe a little too enthusiastically—and let out a breath. "That makes sense. I'll try it as soon as I get home."

"Would you like me to walk you through the process now?"

Ally glanced back at Eve, who was leaning sideways in her wheelchair, propping up her head with her fist, her face full of boredom. "No. I think I've got everything I need."

"Take your time with the incantations, dear," Tess said and stood. "I'm sure you'll do fine."

"Thank you, Professor Caldwell." Ally scooped up the box with both hands and stood.

"Please call me Tess. Your mother would be proud of you."

"Tess," she said and gestured to the box. "I'll return this when I'm done."

"Keep it," Tess said with a generous wave of her hand. "It belongs to you now."

❧ 12 ☙

Ally hurried inside when she got home. She hadn't stopped thinking about the box or what Tess had said since leaving the woman's house. Her thoughts focused on the parchment and the note she had briefly examined the previous day. Now she knew what it was. Now she knew what she needed to do.

On her way to the kitchen table, she flipped the blinds shut and cleared away some of the items she had previously examined from Gabriel's house, along with some of Lucy's drawings.

Tess's words echoed in her mind. "To protect those you love, you must first welcome what they fear."

It all made sense now. All the symbols, the rituals Gabriel had only half understood. Tess had made it clear that the statue itself wasn't evil. It was just a tool, which Gabriel had misused. But she wouldn't follow his path. She would use it in the correct way.

She carefully placed the box on the kitchen table and sat in front of it. This was the moment she had anticipated all the way home. She lifted the lid slowly. The statue, the parchment, the note. They were still there, just as she'd left them. Pulling the items out one by one with great care, she examined each of them reverently before setting them aside.

It would take time to translate everything on the parchment, but it would take even longer to break everything down phonetically to ensure she pronounced them perfectly. On the note Tess had provided to Gabriel, she'd written, "Only speak the correct tongue with correct intentions." Maybe that's where Gabriel had gone wrong. His intentions hadn't been pure. Instead, he'd focused on getting revenge on everyone who'd failed him.

Tess's list of instructions had made no sense before, but now Ally understood all the steps that were laid out along with the list of items she needed to perform the ritual. The words she'd fumbled through earlier, when she'd first received the box from Father Tony, had fallen flat because she hadn't understood their significance. She wouldn't make the same mistake again. Nothing would come out of her mouth until she had done her research. Not a single word, until she was confident that everything was perfect.

According to Tess's note, there were seven key steps to the ritual, and she had all the items in the apartment to perform the ritual. Only the unfamiliar languages stood between her and success.

Using her laptop to help with the translations, she started the process of breaking down everything written on the parchment. Word by word, line by line, she picked it apart, jumping between her laptop's screen, the parchment, and scribbling notes furiously in her notebook.

There were three primary languages written on the parchment: Aramaic, Latin, and something she'd never encountered before called Enochian script. Tess made clear on her personal note to "Only speak the correct tongue."

How the hell is that *going to work?*

Her heart raced a little faster. None of this would be easy. She had *never* spoken any of those languages before. She'd studied some Latin in college, but had always struggled to speak them in the correct tongue. Would saying it close to the original dialect be enough?

Writing out the lines of Latin in her notebook, she followed them with a rough translation.

"Clausa sint viae per quas nox venit.
Custodes ex umbra, exaudi vocem meam.
Fige circulum in carne et sanguine.
Nihil intret, nisi mea voluntate."
"Let the paths by which night comes be closed.
Guardians of shadow, hear my voice.
Fix this circle in flesh and blood.
Let nothing enter, save by my will."

Then painstakingly breaking it down phonetically:

"Clow-zah sint vee-aye pair kwas noks weh-neet.
Koos-toh-dess ex oom-brah, ex-ow-dee voh-chem may-ahm.
Fee-jay cheer-koo-loom in kar-nay et san-gwee-neh.
Nee-hill in-tret, nee-see may-ah voh-loon-tah-tay."

She practiced the words over and over, sounding them out silently until the words rolled off her tongue before moving on to the next verse. Not a single detail on the parchment was missed. She'd even researched the meanings of the symbols and sketches someone had drawn in the margins.

Translating the text took far longer than she had imagined.

By 3 a.m., she was exhausted but ready.

Pushing the kitchen chairs out of the way, she used black powdered charcoal to mark the circle on the floor, drawing the hollow flame sigil and whispering the words slowly. Tess had said intention was everything, and she pushed herself to focus on protection. The image of Lucy popped into her mind. The girl was vulnerable to whatever had attached itself to Nora's family. This ritual seemed like the best way, and possibly the *only* way to protect Nora's family from something so clearly dangerous. There was no telling when it might return.

At each cardinal direction, she placed one of the items from the list: an iron key to the North, a scorched ribbon to the East, created using her father's old lighter and a doll ribbon, a single strand of Lucy's hair to the South—she'd found it stuck within a piece of tape on one of the girl's drawings—and a dried rose to the West.

After taking a deep breath, she sat cross-legged in the center of the circle. Everything was set. Now she just needed to say the words in the correct tongue.

She placed the box in front of her, along with a single candle, and faced the statue.

Lighting the candle, she started to recite the words.

"Koos-toh-dess ex oom-brah..."
"Guardians of shadow, hear my voice..."

The flames were important, it said, to rise as high as a bull's horn. Ally had to look up the length of a bull's horn on the internet—up to fourteen inches, it said. How would she get a flame to rise that high in her little apartment? She was sure it didn't need to *stay* that high for long—a short burst should do, but aside from her father's old lighter, she had nothing to create a flame that would rise more than an inch. Even so, she had disarmed the smoke alarms. The last thing she wanted was for the fire department to show up in the middle of the night and catch her mid-ritual surrounded by occult drawings and symbols etched across the floor.

"Fee-jay cheer-koo-loom in kar-nay..."
"Fix this circle in flesh and blood..."

She pressed her hand over the flame-shaped carving on the box. The surface felt a little warmer than it should have been. Just her heart beating faster, causing the extra heat?

The candle flickered as she spoke the words exactly as Tess had written them, and she had translated them.

"Nee-hill in-tret, nee-see may-ah voh-loon-tah-tay..."
  "Let nothing enter, save by my will..."

Another image of Lucy flashed through her mind—the girl's innocent face. This was not only to guard and protect Nora and Daniel but also Lucy. The one candle in the center burst brighter and the others dimmed as a shadow stretched long around her, the sigil seeming to writhe as she stared at it.

One by one, she spoke the words. Not one mistake. Not one mispronunciation, she was sure.

The ribbon began to smolder, turning black before her eyes, although no flame touched it. Glancing to her right, Lucy's strand of hair was gone. Up in flames? A glance to her left revealed that the iron key was wobbling in place as if some unseen force were trying to grab it unsuccessfully. Behind her, the dried rose had turned to ash.

Something inside the box clicked. Something had shifted.

She stared at it with wide eyes, frozen in her seat, waiting for what might happen next.

The smell of burnt cloth floated through the air around her.

Then, it stopped.

Silence.

The candle's flame died out, and the smoke cleared.

She had come to the end, exhausted and thirsty, but... nothing had changed.

Had she done them correctly? But if so, shouldn't *something* have happened? Tess hadn't mentioned what might happen when she was finished, but it just felt... incomplete.

Opening the box carefully, she found nothing inside.

Her shoulders dropped, and she let out a sigh.

"Shit." She scanned through the notes again. Had she missed

anything? Was there something Tess hadn't told her? Something more to complete, something unspoken?

No. She'd gone through every step. It was correct.

Maybe she'd rushed through it too quickly. Tess had said to take her time with the incantations. But her mind was exhausted after straining to get every detail correct, and she needed sleep. There were only a few hours before she would need to wake up again. Daniel would arrive at 8 a.m. sharp with Lucy in tow to start another phase of the renovations in the parlor. If she didn't go to sleep now, it wasn't going to happen.

Blowing out the candles, she stood and walked to the living room couch. She dropped into the cushions and closed her eyes. Whatever she'd done wrong with the ritual, it would need to wait until morning. As soon as she took a deep breath, the silence buried her in darkness.

❧ 13 ❧

Something wasn't right. Nora stepped into the parlor with her head spinning. How had she gotten there? And why couldn't she remember waking up or even getting ready that morning? It was still dark outside, so what time was it? She checked her pockets for her phone, but they were empty. She hadn't even brought along her purse.

Impossible.

Closing the door behind her, the parlor windows had fogged up. All the lights were off, and she was alone.

"Ally?" Nora called out.

No answer.

A strange smell filled the air, like something burning. Fine particles, like tiny crystals, floated through the air. Not crystals —although they twinkled like tiny stars. Embers—drifting down from the ceiling like snowflakes from hell.

She glanced up. The ceiling was gone, replaced by a thick darkness spewing embers from an unseen source.

She flipped the light switch on the wall. It didn't work.

A blackout?

She headed toward the front desk. Had she mistakenly come in too early? Running her fingers across the empty counter, she yanked away her hand. A thick dust covered everything. Not dust—ash. And the foggy windows. Not fog—smoke.

An eerie silence settled over the parlor until a child's voice came from the hallway. Lucy's voice, small and strained, like she was in pain.

"Lucy?" Nora called.

She hurried around the front desk toward the hallway, her feet slipping through the ash that covered the floor. Smoke rose with each footstep.

Lucy stumbled out of the hallway with her arms extended. Her little fingers brushed against the walls as she moved forward with her face angled up toward the ceiling. Something was wrong. Her eyes were clouded over, and her mouth was hanging open.

Blind?

The lost girl gasped within the thick air.

"Lucy?" Nora rushed to her, dropping onto one knee in front of her, and jostled her to catch her attention. "What's wrong?"

"I can't see anything," Lucy whispered. "It's dark, Mommy. Everything's gone."

"I'm right here." Nora embraced her daughter. Her little body was icy, chilled to the bone. "We'll get you to a doctor. Where's Ally?"

Lucy's eyes watered. "I can't find her."

A sharp cracking noise came from the séance room.

Nora pulled Lucy closer and raced to the doorway of the séance room. A gasp filled her lungs.

Her sister was there, sitting behind the séance table. She was wearing the same outfit Nora used to wear during a psychic reading—the same makeup, the same jewelry—but it was all... wrong. Her head was tilted back like Lucy's, her eyes wide and pure white. Her mouth was closed—sewn shut—and there was blood dripping from her eyes. The blood trickled down over her cheeks and clothes. Her wrists were tied together with rope.

She struggled to speak through the threads of her tightly sewn lips.

Nora gasped in a breath to scream, but it was cut short by something descending from the ceiling. It vaguely resembled a human body dangling upside down, wrapped in a cocoon of twisted hair, but this thing wasn't human. It was an abomination.

Its pale body peeked through the thick layers of hair. Its skin was covered with smoldering embers that escaped into the air through the cracks. The thing twitched and writhed like a butterfly escaping its chrysalis.

A spider broke through a crack in the cocoon and scurried away. Then another.

More streamed out, flowing from every part of its body, until the thing let out an ear-shattering shriek and burst into a thousand pieces. Spiders flew in every direction.

Nora tried to shield her face as the spiders rained down over her arms and face. They scurried past her hands, making their way up to her cheeks, through her hair, and across her eyelids.

While struggling to brush them away, she could only think of Lucy. Where was she? They needed to get out of there. The panic swelled until she let out a deafening scream.

Nora awoke in complete darkness.

She wasn't in bed with Daniel. She wasn't even in her room. Her hot breath filled the air, but she couldn't move. Something massive pressed down on her.

A panicked cry filled her strained throat. Then another.

The back of her head rested painfully against a hard surface. She was on the floor, judging by the creaking of the hardwood floors as her weight shifted.

A familiar scent caught her attention. Lucy.

This was Lucy's room. She was under her daughter's bed. But how the hell had she gotten there?

She struggled to free herself, but the weight of the box spring and mattress on top of her was too much to just push aside. She had no leverage. No way to lift it more than an inch. Turning onto her side wasn't an option, but she could turn her head.

A sliver of light caught her attention. It was coming through the crack along the bottom of Lucy's closed bedroom door.

Was her daughter asleep in the bed above her?

Or was she alone?

Certainly, Lucy would have heard her struggling, heard her cries.

"Lucy," Nora cried out. It might waken her daughter, might frighten her, but what choice did she have? "Mommy's stuck down here. Are you there? Lucy?"

Pushing herself sideways a little at a time, she moved toward the trickle of light.

A breeze swept through the room. Had Lucy left the window open? Memories of her daughter venturing out on the roof to "save" Blanco came flooding back.

"Lucy," Nora said. "I'm trapped under your bed. Can you please get Daddy?"

A stack of her Lucy's drawings stirred on her desk.

Then she froze. A shadow passed through the room.

She wasn't alone.

Something was standing at the foot of Lucy's bed. The silhouette was there, although she couldn't turn far enough to see it clearly.

"Lucy?" Nora called again.

The person took a step, and Nora held her breath.

The floor creaked when it took another step. Then another, until the figure stopped just a little beyond her view. It wasn't Lucy. They were black as midnight against the darkness of her daughter's room. They shifted, then crouched and dropped to the floor until their face filled her view.

A face as ghastly as her worst nightmare peered in at her. Wide black eyes surrounded by flesh that stretched over its bony frame like diseased leather. Its mouth opened in a twisted grin when it spotted her. A putrid stench filled the air. Two horns curled along the sides of its skull. Its nostrils were two gaping holes, and it sniffed at the air.

It reached a bony arm toward her, scraping its claw-like fingers across the floor. It crouched lower and pushed forward, squeezing into the cramped space. The bed shook.

It was trying to climb under the bed with her.

"Lucy! Daniel!" she cried again.

No answer.

She struggled in a frenzy to push away from it.

She couldn't scream. Her voice failed. Her lungs locked, and her throat clenched. Only a single high-pitched whine escaped her throat, rising to a feverish pitch.

"No, no, no!" she finally cried out.

The thing moved forward, dragging itself closer, faster than she could retreat. Its fingers hovered inches from her face. Only a few more moments and it would have her.

The bed shuddered.

It grabbed her arm. Its flesh was like ice against her skin.

She screamed.

Pulling against it with all her strength, she couldn't feel her arm anymore. It had gone numb.

She jerked back, but it yanked her closer toward its gaping mouth.

Where is Daniel? And Lucy?

Had the thing already come for them?

Her head bumped against something on the floor. Not the creature this time. A metal object. Her cheek rested against its cool surface for a moment. One of Lucy's toys? Or Blanco's?

Without thinking, she twisted around just enough to grab it. Her fingers swept over its surface, and her mind painted a clear picture of it now.

The crucifix. The one Father Tony had given her.

But how had it ended up under Lucy's bed?

Gripping it like a hammer, she swung the top section down against the creature's fingers. The reaction was immediate. When the metal touched its skin, the creature released her and lurched back. The release provided a moment to breathe, but it still hovered at the side of the bed, watching her with a wide grin. Was it just playing with her?

She could see the creature's face better from that angle. Its twisted, torn flesh filled the space between eyes, openings, and teeth—all of it churning within the darkness as if it hadn't yet settled on which nightmare it intended to manifest. It shuddered within the darkness and then faded.

Another face came into view. This one was clear. Not the horrid thing she'd seen moments earlier.

Lucy's sweet face.

Her daughter's eyes were wide with terror.

"Mommy?" Lucy asked.

Nora collapsed, dropping the crucifix onto the floor and letting out a full breath at the same time. "Yes. It's me, sweetheart."

"I was scared."

"I'm sorry," Nora said. "I'm *so* sorry. I was scared too."

Nora inched herself sideways out from under the bed, scraping her elbows along the way. Near the edge, Lucy reached in to help, her little arms extending toward her like the creature had done moments earlier. Nora pretended to accept her daughter's help, but there was nothing Lucy could do in the physical sense.

Daniel rushed into the room a moment later. He flipped on the light and stared at them with wide eyes. "What's going on?"

The humiliation of Daniel seeing her climb out from under Lucy's bed sent a fresh wave of panic through her. He would think she'd lost her mind... and maybe she had. How could she explain any of it?

Nora climbed to her feet and then sat on the edge of the bed.

The crucifix was still in her hand, but she slipped it under a fold in the blanket so Daniel wouldn't ask about it.

The window was open. Just a crack, but a wave of fresh air blew in around them.

"Why is the window open?" Daniel stepped across the room and closed it.

Nora cried. She couldn't help it.

"Are you okay?" Daniel sat down beside her.

Nora nodded.

"Do you want to talk about it?" he asked.

Nora shook her head.

"Then, we won't."

Ten minutes later, her heart slowed to a normal rhythm. She stood again, taking the crucifix with her. While Daniel tucked Lucy back into bed, Nora slipped the crucifix into the top drawer of Lucy's dresser. She could retrieve it the next day.

After leaving Lucy's room, an odd smell lingered in the air. Nobody had commented on it, but it was definitely there.

The sickening stench of burning flesh and rot.

$$\text{❧}\quad 14 \quad \text{❧}$$

The next morning, Nora was still reeling from what had happened the night before. She'd barely slept. The questions had piled up in her mind, and she needed answers. She'd spent the night trying to process what had happened but had kept it all to herself. Who could she talk to about her nightmarish encounter? Ally would listen with an open mind, but she wouldn't have answers. Only one other person came to mind.

Father Tony.

On a Monday morning he wouldn't be at the church. She texted him, hoping he'd get her message. He texted back a few minutes later with the invitation to come right over.

Daniel agreed to watch Lucy while she needed to "take care of something important." He didn't argue, complain, or ask questions. Not after last night.

After getting ready, she headed out the door to see the priest.

The drive to his house didn't take long. She parked on the street, stepped up to his porch, and rang the doorbell. After a long pause, the door swung open and Father Tony stood in the doorway dressed in slacks and a flannel shirt.

He broke into a wide smile and then opened the door a little more. "I didn't expect to see you again so soon."

"Sorry for the short notice," Nora said, "but something happened."

His expression changed to concern. "I hope it's nothing serious."

"It could have been," she said. "I'm hoping you can help me make sense of it."

"I can try." Father Tony gestured for her to come in.

She followed him inside. The shotgun was there, beside the door—the same one he'd used in Gabriel's house months earlier. It reminded her of how close they'd come to disaster, and the stakes of venturing too close to the occult.

Father Tony led her over to the living room. He sat in a recliner while she took a seat on the couch across from him. The TV was on, quietly playing in the background, and he clicked it off as soon as she sat down. The sudden silence was a bit unnerving, but at least she had his full attention.

"What can I help you with?" he asked.

"I'm not sure exactly where to start," she said. "I seem to keep having strange things happen to me. I'd like to say that things got better after you gave me the crucifix, but I'm afraid things are getting worse."

He listened with a solemn expression. "No need to hold anything back."

"That's exactly why I came here. You're the only person I feel would understand. Remember when I was attacked in the parking lot?"

"Yes."

"Well, something similar happened... but worse."

He swallowed. "I see."

"I woke up under my daughter's bed."

His eyebrows went up, and he studied her for a moment. "Sleepwalking?"

"I suppose it's something like that—except I've never done anything like that before if my life. It was terrifying enough to wake up in that position, but then... someone was there in the room with me, while I was trapped under her bed. He didn't go after Lucy. He attacked *me*. They weren't human. They were demonic, I'm sure."

"How do you know?"

"I saw its face this time." She winced. The nightmarish images flashed through her mind. "Its eyes—it didn't have eyes. Just empty black sockets. The thing was grabbing at me, trying to drag me out from under her bed. God only knows how I managed to squeeze under there in the first place, or what possessed me to be there. But the only thing that stopped the attack was a crucifix that you gave me. I don't know how it got there under the bed—I must have carried it with me."

He nodded again but kept silent.

"Do you think it might have something to do with Gabriel?" Nora asked. "Do you think his spirit might still be here somehow?"

"Not him. Not from your description." Father Tony stood suddenly. "Let me show you something."

He led her to the kitchen and gestured to the table before walking to the closet, pulling out a worn blue notebook, and bringing it over to her. They sat across from each other, dropping the notebook between them. It was nothing out of the ordinary, but the edges were curled as if someone had used it a lot. He pushed it toward her.

"This is Gabriel's last notebook," he said. "Everything he didn't want anyone else to see. I've given you and Ally most of the occult items from Gabriel's house, but not everything. I held onto this because I don't feel it's... finished."

"What do you mean, finished?"

"Finished, meaning I haven't figured it out yet." He nudged it toward her. "These were his last thoughts, the last people he talked to before he died. I couldn't bring myself to get rid of it. Not yet."

Nora opened it and flipped through the pages. There were notes, sketches, numbers, and diagrams. Hundreds of random details scribbled across every page. Everything in it revolved around the occult.

"One thing I've learned while going through his house," Father Tony said, "is that he'd gone deeper down that rabbit hole than anyone could have guessed. You were just the last medium he'd contacted before committing the final horrible act with his pets in front of his fireplace. He'd been planning this thing for a long time before you ever met him, and I think he got help from someone."

"Who?"

"That's what I'm trying to figure out," he said. "Gabriel wasn't knowledgeable about such things. Someone must have stepped in and provided him with at least some of this information. He was a veterinarian, not someone well-versed in the occult. It's not common knowledge. *I* sure as hell didn't give it to him. I'm sure he gathered at least some of it off the internet, but judging by the documents and items I found in his house, he hadn't just dabbled in a little black magic. He'd jumped headfirst into it—swam straight to the gates of hell to get what he wanted."

"You think this is connected to what happened to me?"

He tilted his head. "It's hard to say, but... we shouldn't rule it out. It's possible."

"Then why... me?"

"Perhaps he'd already targeted you prior to your last confrontation at his house—not only by attacking you through his spirit, but by enlisting something else."

"Another malevolent spirit?"

"Maybe," he said, "but judging by your description he might have evoked a greater evil."

"A demon?"

"Yes."

Nora considered it for a moment. "Actually, that makes sense. I know what I saw last night, and this is the first time things have made sense."

"You came here for answers, but I'm afraid I don't have many," Father Tony said. "Not yet. And I don't know how to stop it."

Nora grinned. "But aren't you a..."

"Yes, I'm a priest, but contrary to what you might believe, most priests are not experts in all things demonic. We don't go out chasing demons in our spare time—" He met her gaze and grinned. "—although it seems things are certainly headed in that direction for me. You might want to call someone with expertise in these kinds of things. I can speak to the bishop's office. I'm sure they'll know who to send."

Nora shook her head. "Won't that take a lot of time? And they'll investigate everything, won't they? My business, my family —it'll all turn into one big investigation instead of helping."

"It might take some time," he admitted, "but the sooner you start—"

"No." She frowned. "I don't want to go down that road. My family's at risk. This can't wait."

"I understand." He nodded sympathetically. "I would offer to stop by your house this morning, but unfortunately, I have another family to attend to that can't wait. Wait—perhaps later this afternoon?"

She met his gaze with a spark of hope. "Yes. I'd like that."

"I'll call when I can give you a specific time to stop by."

"Thank you, Father," she said. "I probably should have accepted your previous offer."

"No worries," he said. "In the meantime, keep your family close. Avoid isolation and avoid anything that might invite unwanted influence from the spirit world. I know that's your business, but if we can reduce the vulnerabilities."

"I will." Nora closed the notebook. "Thank you for letting me see this. It helps me understand better what I'm dealing with." She hesitated to hand it back. "Can I borrow it?"

He stared at it and swallowed. "Under the circumstances, yes. I suppose I should have given it to Ally when she stopped by earlier. I just needed a little more time to go through it. My curiosity kept me from handing it over."

"I understand," she said.

"Speaking of Ally, did she dispose of the box I gave to her yet?"

"The books, you mean?"

"The box." Father Tony looked confused. "The wooden box."

"I don't remember seeing a box."

Father Tony pressed his lips together, and his face tightened. "She didn't show it to you or tell you about it?"

Nora shook her head. "She didn't say anything about a box."

He narrowed his eyes. "Nothing? She promised to get rid of it by the end of the day. That was yesterday."

"I'll talk to her when I get home."

"Please do that." He reached across the table and crossed his fingers over hers. "Make sure she doesn't open it. Destroy it. I told her that. It's not... safe. I would take care of it myself, but it's not so easy for a man my age to take care of much anymore."

Nora's mind raced back to the moment when Ally had walked into the parlor after her visit with Father Tony.

Books, Ally had said. That's what she said she'd picked up from Father Tony this time.

The last of Gabriel's occult items.

Books.

Ally hadn't mentioned anything about a wooden box. Why wouldn't she have said *something* about it?

Nora stood, clutching the notebook with both hands. "Don't worry. I'll make sure she takes care of it. Today."

$$\text{❧ 15 ❧}$$

Nora stepped into the parlor and was immediately met by Daniel's exhausted face. He was patching up a broken section of tile on the floor while Lucy and Blanco played in the corner. Blanco was curled up on a rug, while Lucy crawled on her hands and knees, giggling as she scurried around him.

"Where's Ally?" she asked.

"You tell me." He didn't look at her. "I haven't seen her all morning."

"She's not helping you?"

He shook his head.

"Lucy," Nora said. "Have you seen Ally today?"

"No, Mommy," Lucy answered.

Nora turned away and walked down the hallway toward Ally's apartment. She stopped at the door and stared at it a moment. Ally's car was in the parking lot. She was home, but it was almost noon.

If she'd gone for a walk, wouldn't she have said something?

She knocked.

"Ally?" she said.

Silence.

She twisted the doorknob. It was unlocked, so she opened the door and stepped inside.

The lights were off. Nothing moved. No sign of Ally. The place still smelled like her father's cigarettes, and the memories came flooding back. She didn't like coming in here. Not anymore. Even after Ally had cleared out most of their father's old furniture and made the place her own.

Ally had redecorated, adding her own touches, but she hadn't taken down the wallpaper yet. Their parents had loved that outdated '8os pattern, but it would all have to go. They would renovate the entire apartment, one day, but Ally needed a place to stay—something cheap—and they had bills to pay, so it all had worked out. She'd agreed to move in. That was the deal. Renovations would come later.

Nora flipped on the lights. The blinds were raised over the windows, but the light streaming in was a dull gray because of the clouds. An odd scent hung in the air. Candles? She didn't see anything burning now, but maybe Ally lit one earlier that morning.

"Ally?"

No answer.

She wasn't one to snoop, but Father Tony's warning about the box still hung in her mind. It had to be there somewhere, unless Ally had kept her word to dispose of it. But something didn't feel right about the situation. It still bothered her that Ally hadn't said anything about it.

Her gaze turned toward the kitchen. She spotted something on the kitchen table.

There it was.

She hurried over and flipped on the lights above the table. It was everything she had imagined, by the way Father Tony had described it: a wooden antique box marked with occult symbols etched into the lid and sides. It was far older than any antique she'd ever seen—almost ancient.

One symbol caught her attention—something darkly familiar. She'd seen it before, in a book or in a nightmare. The same jagged arcs surrounded by what looked like an open flame with a hollow center, like an eye.

She couldn't help but stare at it. The etched symbols across its lid held an almost divine presence, like some sacred religious relic. Nora leaned in and touched the wood. It was cold but seemed to connect with her on some deeper level.

Father Tony had explicitly told them not to open the box, but something pulled at her. It called to her.

Just a peek inside.

She opened the box. A stone statue of a demon stared back at her, sitting beside a yellowed parchment and another item that seemed out of place among the others—a folder sheet of white paper.

Removing only the paper, she scanned the handwriting. It outlined detailed instructions for a ritual. A woman had written it, but not Ally. She placed it back inside the box and closed the lid.

One of Ally's notebooks was sitting beside the box. Nora opened it and flipped through the pages. Her sister had translated various lines of what looked like Latin into English and then had broken the lines down phonetically.

So she could say them out loud.

For a ritual.

One name jumped out at her.

Moloch.

She closed the notebook and glanced down. The hollow flame symbol was there on the floor, drawn inside a large charcoal circle—the same symbol as the one on the box. A burnt candle sat in the center, and bits of ashes lay scattered around its edges.

That's where the smell of a candle had come from. She had burned something there recently—maybe even that morning.

And there was also a colorful scattering of construction paper, crayons, and pencils on the floor. Lucy's artwork. It would have warmed her heart under any normal situation, except her daughter's designs and drawings were far from her usual creations. Instead of rainbows, cats, and butterflies, she'd drawn a massive figure with twisted horns standing above a child while flames burned around them. A structure towered behind them— she'd labeled it "black-eyed house." A smaller stick figure, unmistakably Lucy, stood near the bottom. Her daughter had labeled it carefully in block letters: "ME."

Nora gasped. It was wrong, both on a maternal and deeper level.

Lucy had drawn that. *Her* daughter—*her* child—had imagined this thing. Or worse, had she seen it? Had Ally instructed her on what to draw or even shown her through books or visualizations what the symbols meant and where they had come from?

The anger swelled into a rage. Not only had Ally broken her promise to dispose of the box, but it looked like she'd used it as part of a ritual. She wanted to scream in that moment until a realization hit her.

How could she blame Ally?

Lucy had grown up in that world. And Nora and her sister had both done the same thing, having been immersed in the occult all their lives. How could she blame her sister for passing along the same information, stories, and tales that their father had passed along to them, and his parents had passed along to him? It went back generations. It was their *heritage*. The occult and spiritualism had surrounded Lucy all her life, and this is all she'd known.

Turning back to the box, she calmed a bit, if only to process everything. It was clear. They had to get rid of the box, not only to keep their word to Father Tony, but for Lucy's sake.

Nora stepped away from the table, but before she could turn around, Ally's tired voice cut through the silence.

"Nora?" Ally asked. "What are you doing in my apartment?"

❧ 16 ❧

Ally woke to a noise in her apartment. It was coming from the kitchen—thumping footsteps moving across the tiled floor. Lucy? Maybe Nora?

Sunlight streamed into her bedroom, warming the edge of her face. Her mind was clear, but only for a moment. How long had she slept? What time was it?

She sat up suddenly and checked the time on her phone next to her bed. 11:35 a.m.

"Shit." Panic swept through her. She jumped out of bed and scrambled to get dressed. She rarely overslept. Daniel would be pissed, Nora concerned, and Lucy disappointed.

The ritual she'd performed the previous night had failed spectacularly. She must have said the wrong words or not gone far enough with them before giving up. All the possible errors flooded her mind. Whatever the reason, she would need to talk with Tess again before attempting it again.

After grabbing her phone, she stepped out of the room. Nora was there, standing next to the kitchen table, staring down at the charcoal circle she'd drawn on the floor. Ally's heart skipped a beat. Her sister wasn't supposed to see any of that, not yet. How would she explain what she had done?

"Nora?" she asked. "What are you doing in my apartment?"

Nora turned sharply and met her gaze. There was fear on her sister's face, but more anger than anything.

"What is all of this?" Nora demanded.

"I was going to tell you." Ally swallowed.

"When? It looks like you've already spent a lot of time going through it... with Lucy too."

"I'm just... trying out some things I found."

"Stuff you found? That's the box Father Tony gave you, isn't it?"

"Yes." Ally paused. "He gave me a lot of stuff. You know that."

"But he told you to get rid of the box."

"How do you know what he said?" Ally studied her sister's expression, looking for answers.

"Because I stopped by to see him yesterday, and he asked about it."

"Now you're spying on me?"

"Nobody's spying on you, Ally." Nora stepped forward, folding her arms over her chest. "I was worried about you. Why aren't you out there helping Daniel? Lucy also asked about you. What's going on?"

"I was up late last night." Ally brushed the hair out of her eyes.

Nora gestured to the chalk drawing on the floor. "Doing this?"

There was no point in denying it, but she couldn't tell her sister everything. Not yet.

"I was working through some translations, trying to figure out their exact meaning. Sometimes you don't grasp the complete understanding of something until you put it into practice. I've always worked like that—immersing myself in it. You know that."

"Father Tony trusted you."

"And I won't betray his trust."

Nora stared at the box. "He was very concerned about this box in particular because of its connection to Gabriel."

Ally followed her sister's gaze. "I understand, but I swear... I haven't done anything with it."

"It sure looks like you have." Nora glanced down at the candle and ashes.

"It's just... research." Along with Ally's brief explanation came a nagging voice. It called out from the back of her mind. Her sister was right. She'd already crossed the line, and even worse, it was possible that something she'd done—something she'd released earlier—had allowed the attack to happen. The guilt sent a chill up her spine, but she quickly pushed it away. No, whatever had gone wrong, there was still time to fix it. It was nothing she couldn't handle.

Nora shook her head. "This isn't just research. This looks like something Gabriel might do."

"No." Ally held up her hands. "This is *way* different from anything Gabriel did. I'm careful... I know what I'm doing. Father Tony doesn't need to worry about me."

"*I'm* a little worried. Why would you even play around with something like this?"

"For you." Ally stepped forward. "And Lucy."

Nora furrowed her brow, her lips parted in a mix of confusion and disbelief. "What are you talking about?"

"Just hear me out," Ally said. "I think we both know that what happened to you in the parking lot wasn't natural. Maybe it's connected to something that Gabriel did months ago, something that got left behind, or maybe it's connected to the ritual he performed in his house before he ended his life, but there *is* something dark going on here. Can't you feel it? Something attached itself to us or is targeting us."

Nora hesitated before answering. Her expression turned solemn, and her shoulders dropped. "Yes. I feel it too. Last night I woke up under Lucy's bed—God only knows why—and something attacked me in the darkness. I'm scared, Ally. That's one of the reasons I came in here. Things *are* getting worse."

Ally stared into her sister's eyes then glanced down at her clothes. "Are you okay?"

"I had Father Tony's crucifix with me," she said. "It worked."

"I'm sorry." Ally held back a rising urge to embrace her sister. Maybe it was the guilt rising to the surface again, but if she had somehow caused all of this, then she had to do everything in her power to stop it. She couldn't give up now. "I've been up all night trying to figure out how to protect all of us from what I believe is still here."

"By toying with all the same things that fueled Gabriel's insanity?" Nora shook her head. "I saw the statue in the box. That's a demon. You should know that."

"It's not what you think," Ally said. "I'm not forming any alliances with any demons—that's ridiculous—I'm forming a shield around our family, to keep them away."

Nora stared into her eyes. "Whatever happened out there, it's not what you think it is. Either way, you need to keep your promise to Father Tony and get rid of that box... *today*."

Ally nodded slowly. "I will."

A moment later, Daniel stepped into the doorway and frowned at Ally.

"So you *are* alive." His skin glistened with sweat, and his shoulders slumped. "Where have you been? I could have used some help this morning."

"Sorry," Ally said. "I overslept."

Blanco came in right behind him, prancing forward and stopping at Daniel's feet. His tail was up, with his gaze fixed on the kitchen. He hissed.

"Now you've got Blanco mad," he said.

Ally followed the cat's gaze. No signs of anything unusual. Maybe he smelled the burnt candle from the failed ritual.

"Daniel?" Nora asked. "Where's Lucy?"

Daniel glanced back down the hall toward the parlor. "I left her playing in the parlor."

"Without Blanco?" Nora asked.

He shrugged. "She's not with him all the time."

"No," Nora said. "She *is* with him all the time."

Ally stepped toward the door, and then Nora did the same. They hurried out of the apartment and toward the front parlor with Daniel following them.

"Lucy?" Ally called out. "Your favorite aunt is awake now. What are you up to?"

When they walked into the front room, Nora gasped, and Daniel let out a heavy sigh.

Lucy was facing the wall, and a red crayon dropped from her hand when they walked in. Orange, red, and black crayons lay scattered on the floor below a crude sketch on the wall in the unmistakable hand of a child. It was similar to what Lucy had drawn in Ally's apartment. The image was almost identical. A horned figure with its eyes gouged out stood in a sea of flames. Smaller stick figures kneeled in front of the figure, the fires circling them like a cage. A tall, narrow house stood behind them with the words "black-eyed house" below it. One figure resembled Lucy, with her arms outstretched toward the horned figure as if waiting to accept its embrace.

Lucy had scrawled something else below everything in bright red, jagged capital letters.

MOLOCH.

Daniel's mouth fell open. "What the hell is this?"

Nora couldn't say anything. She stared at the strange drawings with the same question running through her mind. They were *exactly* like the drawings she'd seen in Ally's apartment, the ones Lucy had drawn, only larger and with more detail.

"I'll get some soap and water." Ally glanced around nervously. "Or we can paint over it."

"I'm not worried about having to paint over it, Ally," Daniel said. "That's not the issue here. Please tell me why Lucy is drawing stuff like this. And don't try to explain it away as just a kid being a kid."

"I'm sorry," Lucy said, taking a step back. She was holding something in her hands behind her back, and a bit of red crayon was smeared across the front of her dress. They had literally caught her red-handed.

Nora dropped in front of her daughter, blocking Daniel's view of her, and spoke in a soft, steady voice. "Why did you draw that, honey?"

Lucy shrugged. "It's just something I thought of."

"*That's* what I'm talking about," Daniel said as if the answer were clear. He turned to face Ally and pointed at her. "You're filling her mind with all this—"

"I'm not," Ally cut in. "She hears stories."

"From whom?"

"From..." Ally gestured to the space around them. "... life."

Nora stood. "What do you want her to do, Daniel? We can't keep this away from her forever. It's part of her heritage. She's going to learn about everything we do at some point."

"I get it," he said. "And we're not going to have this argument again, but she shouldn't be exposed to stuff like this—not yet. Not at eight years old."

"I'm sorry," Lucy said again, and her eyes watered.

"I know you're sorry," Nora said to her in a soft voice. "But you should never draw anything on the walls. Pictures go in your notebook. Understand?"

Lucy nodded.

"Again," Daniel said, "it's not what she did. It's what she *drew*. This isn't the stuff an eight-year-old mind creates—not rainbows and unicorns. Don't tell me it's just her wild imagination. This isn't... normal."

"I don't know what it is," Nora said, "but she's just drawing what she saw in a book or something."

Daniel looked at Lucy with more fear than anger on his face. "Where did you see this before?"

Lucy cowered a bit then shrugged.

"In one of the books here?" he asked. "In Ally's apartment?"

Lucy shook her head.

"Maybe she had a nightmare." Nora glanced at Ally for a moment and then looked away. "Like the one I did."

"You mean what happened last night?" Daniel asked.

"Yes, when you found me under Lucy's bed. I don't remember crawling under there, and I barely remember falling asleep. But when I opened my eyes, it wasn't you and Lucy coming to wake me up. I'd already been awake for a few minutes at that point, and there was something in the dark, watching me."

Ally stepped forward. "Why didn't you tell me about this?"

Nora scoffed and countered, "Why didn't you tell me about Lucy's drawings? And the box that Father Tony gave you, the one you were supposed to destroy?"

Daniel looked at Nora and then at Ally. "What's going on here? Both of you are keeping secrets now? Is that what's going on in our lives?" He shook his head suddenly. "It doesn't matter." He gestured to Ally. "Lucy's not staying with you anymore. She will never go in there again. Not for a second."

"Daniel, I—" Ally stammered.

"No." He grabbed Lucy's jacket from the hook by the door. "You've always had one foot in that world: rituals, symbols, the occult. I never said anything before because you always justified it as research for your profession here, but this is different. She's just a child, and I don't want you filling her head with it anymore."

He stormed out a moment later, Lucy in tow, the bell above the parlor door jingling louder than normal, and the door slammed shut behind him.

Silence filled the parlor until Nora let out her breath.

"I don't blame him," Ally said. "I don't blame either of you for getting mad at me. You don't understand."

Nora turned and stared at the drawing on the wall. "What I saw last night in Lucy's bedroom, it looked just like that."

"That's not possible." Ally shook her head.

"What's not possible?"

"That you both saw the same thing."

"Why not?"

Ally hesitated before answering. "Because you're... protected."

"Protected from what? Stop playing games and tell me what's going on."

"I'm sorry I didn't tell you." Ally glanced at the floor. "I knew both of you would be upset if you found out, but it's not exactly easy to talk with you about this stuff, after all that's happened here. You've stepped away from the darker aspect of our business, for good reason, and Daniel seems to think it's all just theatrics."

"This has something to do with the box I found in your apartment?"

Ally nodded. "But it's not what you think."

"Father Tony told you to destroy it."

"I will destroy it," she said. "Just not today."

Nora folded her arms across her chest. "Why not?"

"I need more time."

"Time for what?"

"Time to understand it." Ally showed a bit of exasperation on her face. "And I'm not sure it'll make any sense to you either."

"Try me."

"Are you sure?" Ally scanned her sister's face. "It's... dark."

"Dark like the stuff Gabriel was involved with?"

She nodded. "But I swear..." Ally gestured to the apartment. "The research I've done in there... It's for your protection. Nothing nefarious."

Nora's eyes widened. "My protection? Protection from what? Please just tell me what you've done."

"I think you already know," Ally said. "Something's still here. A dark entity—something Gabriel released—and now it's targeting us."

Nora looked into her sister's eyes for a long time, then she nodded. "I know."

Her sister cautiously continued, "Gabriel is gone, but what he left behind is far worse. He performed a ritual, made sacrifices to the demon Moloch, to see his daughter again. But the ritual... he messed it up."

"How do you know all this?"

"I found the instructions in the box. The ritual required precise pronunciation, precise timing, precise... everything. He couldn't have done all that without extensive research, which I'm sure he didn't do. He only completed the first part, which opened the door for other lesser demons to enter this world. Not Moloch, but... just as awful." Ally glanced toward Lucy's drawings. "Is that really the same figure you saw in your house?"

Nora nodded. "Very similar."

"That's not Moloch."

"Then who... *what* is it?"

"I don't know yet, but that's why I need to do this," she said, "for you and Lucy and even Daniel, although he would never believe it."

They were silent for a few seconds. "What does it want?" Nora asked.

"I'm not sure yet, but it seems to target your family. I stayed up all night to do the protection ritual. That's why I was AWOL this morning. That's where the drawing on the floor came from."

Nora's eyes went wide. "You were doing the same ritual that Gabriel tried?"

Ally held up her hands defensively and shook her head. "Not the same," she said. "I did it the *right* way—for your protection. I would do anything to protect you and Lucy, and even Daniel. And this is the only way."

"Are you sure?" Nora's face warmed. "After what happened with Gabriel, how can you think this was a good idea?"

"I'm not like you, Nora. I'm—"

"What?" Nora cut in. "*Real?* Is that what you were going to say? You're not a fraud like me?"

"I wasn't going to say that."

"But you were thinking it."

Ally shook her head. "I can do this."

"Maybe you can," Nora said. "You *are* authentic. I don't have the skills, and I'm sure it's nothing I can ever learn. But I thought we agreed we wouldn't mess with this kind of stuff anymore."

"You make it sound like I'm doing something evil, like I'm playing with fire in the same way Gabriel did."

"From what Father Tony said, you *are* playing with fire," Nora said. "You can't keep the box. We need to get rid of it. Tonight."

Ally paused before responding, "That would be a *huge* mistake."

A noise came from down the hall from Ally's apartment. The cry of an animal in pain.

They both looked at each other at the same time.

"Blanco?" Ally said.

They scrambled toward the apartment together. A wave of dread spread through Nora's chest.

"Didn't Lucy take him with her?" Nora asked.

Ally ran faster without answering, and she arrived in the apartment first, stopping just inside the door to flip on the kitchen lights.

Blanco was there, lying motionless on the kitchen table with smoke rising from his white fur. At first, Nora thought the cat had somehow caught himself on fire.

He let out another sharp, pained cry that pierced the air as they ran to his side. He was slowly moving forward, clawing at the air as if struggling to reach the box. Smoke rose from the branded symbol on his side, and blood oozed from the scars. The injury was bright red, as if the tragic event had happened only minutes ago.

When they'd left the apartment earlier, the box was closed.

Now it was open.

And the statue was lying on its side, facing Blanco with outstretched arms and wide eyes as if welcoming a fresh sacrifice.

꧁ 18 ꧂

Nora reached out to touch Blanco's limp body, but she stopped herself. Waves of heat radiated from his skin. "He's burning up."

Blood soaked the cat's fur and pooled near his paws. He stared up lazily at them.

Ally's face was pale. "No. He can't be dying." She raced away to the bathroom, coming back seconds later with a handful of towels.

"What did you do?" Nora asked, forcing herself to stay calm while stroking the back of Blanco's neck.

"I didn't do anything to him!" Ally said louder than necessary.

They lifted him together, carefully placing him on one of the towels. He barely moved as Ally put another towel beneath him, then scooped him up and held him against her chest.

"We'll take him to the vet," Nora said.

Ally shook her head. "We can't."

"Why not? I'm not just going to sit back and let him die."

"That's not what I mean," Ally said. "We can't take him to the vet looking like this. They'll ask what happened. They'll think we did it—we abused him or something."

The realization hit Nora like a punch to the gut, but her sister was right.

Nora glanced around. "What kind of medical supplies do you have?"

"Nothing for something like this."

"Father Tony," Nora said. "He'll have supplies, I'm sure."

"But how are we going to explain this to *him*?" Ally asked.

Nora shook her head. "We won't have to. He'll understand. He's the only one who will."

They rushed to get Blanco into the car without injuring him further. Nora cradled him like a newborn in the towels, but the blood was already seeping through the bottom, smearing across her fingers. She couldn't stop thinking about how he might bleed to death. She was just thankful that Lucy wasn't there to witness it.

Ally grabbed an extra towel on the way out but paused near the door. "We should bring the—"

"What?" Nora slowed but didn't stop. "What did we forget?"

Before Ally could answer, she rushed back inside and returned a short time later with a few more towels, stacked above a familiar object—the box. "We might need it."

"For what?" Nora held back her frustration, but there wasn't time to argue. She let out an exasperated sigh while rushing across the parking lot toward the car. "Keep that *thing* away from Blanco. Put it in the trunk—all the way to the back."

Nora didn't bother putting him in his carrier this time, but they brought it along. After they'd climbed into the car, she handed off the cat to Ally, who held him in her arms all the way to Father Tony's house. Nora considered calling him, if only to give him a heads-up, but she couldn't decide how she might explain what had happened.

❧

When they arrived at the front door, Father Tony answered on the second knock. When he saw Blanco and the blood, he swung the door open wide and gestured forward.

"Get him inside," Father Tony said, moving quickly despite his age. "You caught me just in time. I was just about to leave for your house, for the blessing."

He didn't ask questions. Ally laid Blanco on the kitchen counter as Father Tony hurried away to a closet around the corner, returning a moment later with a medical emergency bag. Emptying the whole thing onto the kitchen table, he dug through the pile of bandages, gauze, and medications, picking out the ones he needed.

"I have some leftover prescription antibiotics," he said. "I took some of it from Gabriel's house, for my cats. Always have a bag like this. Always be prepared."

Father Tony unfurled the towel around Blanco and inspected the bloody scars. The cat let out a whimper, but something was different—the scars had faded in color, and he wasn't bleeding anymore.

"What happened?" Father Tony finally asked.

Ally and Nora exchanged a glance. "We're not sure," Ally said.

Father Tony looked over at her with a skeptical glance. "He just started bleeding... spontaneously?"

"Yes."

Still watching Ally's face, he continued, "When did it start?"

"About half an hour ago." Nora's body tensed. There was no judgment in his face, but she desperately wanted him to do something—*anything*.

Father Tony turned back to Blanco. "There's no sign of trauma. Could be internal bleeding, but I'm no doctor."

Nora hesitated to ask, "Should we take him to the vet?"

"What would you tell them?" Father Tony asked.

Nora shook her head. "I'm not sure."

"You can take him there, if you have to, but this is... odd." He looked at the scars again, even touching the edge of one with his finger. Blanco didn't recoil. "All this blood came from this little guy?"

They nodded. "Yes," Ally said.

"Very odd. There are no open wounds." He examined Blanco from every angle. "Are you sure he didn't cough it up? Or maybe it came out the other end?"

"It came from his scars," Nora said.

He nodded as if he understood, then stared at Ally with narrowed eyes. "You got rid of that box I gave you, right?"

Ally closed her mouth and pressed her lips together before answering. "I didn't have time."

Father Tony's expression changed. Anger and frustration erupted on his face. "Dammit, I was crystal clear with you."

"I'll do it today," she said, but he seemed not to hear her.

"Forgive me for cursing, but..." He pressed against the sides of his forehead and squeezed. "I shouldn't have given it to you. I shouldn't have trusted you, but after I couldn't get it to burn in the fireplace, I didn't want it in my house or to bring it into the church. Carrying an object like that into my office wouldn't look good, in my position. I didn't even want to try a second time—maybe it would bring something worse."

"There's still time," Nora said. "We brought it with us."

His eyes widened. "You brought it *back*? Why?"

"For protection," Ally answered confidently.

Father Tony looked astounded and perplexed by her answer. "Just don't bring it inside. You can see it's having an adverse effect on him."

Ally stared down at the bloodied towels. "I see that now."

He clenched his teeth, then used rubbing alcohol and gauze to start cleaning up the mess. Blanco squirmed during the process, but at least the bleeding had stopped.

"He's drawn to it," Father Tony said to Ally. "That's another reason why I needed you to get rid of it right away. It was hard enough keeping him away from it while he was here. Whatever

Gabriel did, there's still a connection between this cat and the box."

"I didn't know," Ally said.

"And it's better that you didn't know," he said. "I told you Blanco escaped that night when Gabriel tried to sacrifice him like he did with the dogs, but that's not entirely true. Blanco got outside, maybe while trying to escape, but then he must have turned back. I heard him howling all the way from my house—an awful cry. When I found him near the back door, he was trying to get back *inside* the house, clawing at the door, if you can believe that. He didn't even want me to get near him when I first tried to pick him up. He even tried to bite me—attacked me. At first, I couldn't even move him out of the way to open the door. He just wanted to get back inside. But I pounded on the door and waited... That's when I knew something was wrong. The door was open, so I went in, and the smell hit me—the smell of blood and... burning flesh. That's when I found Gabriel and his dogs..." His voice trailed off.

He continued, "Gabriel did something to that cat. I'm not sure to what degree, but he has a sixth sense about the box, always tracking it down wherever I tried to hide it. I thought if I gave it to you..."

"I'm sorry," Ally said.

"It's not your fault." He looked into her eyes until his shoulders sagged and he looked down. "Forgive me. I shouldn't have put such a heavy burden on you. I thought if I enlisted help from someone with your background, the problem would miraculously go away, but I can see that's not the case. This is my cross to bear, I'm afraid. It's not something I should have handed off to anyone else. I'll take it from here and destroy it the right way. I see now I should have faced the problem as soon as I recognized it. Even priests fear the unknown sometimes."

"What's the right way?" Ally asked.

He met her gaze with a confused expression. "What do you mean?"

"What's the right way to destroy it? You suggested I smash it or dispose of it. Is there another way?"

He shook his head slowly. "Priests are expected to have all the answers, but... I'm not sure, in this case."

"Regarding an exorcism," Nora said, "you mentioned before about speaking to someone in the bishop's office?"

He nodded slowly and then pushed his lips together. "It would take time, as well as the high probability that it wouldn't be approved. Exorcisms are generally reserved for people, they would point out, not antique wooden boxes."

"What if we don't get approval?" Nora asked.

"You would need it," he said.

"But this is an emergency," Nora said. "What would it take to perform an exorcism *today*? Is there a way to get around all the bureaucracy? I can't bring it home—I won't—and Blanco may die if we don't do something. We need to destroy it—exorcise it —today."

Father Tony seemed to ponder the thought for a moment. "There *is* another option. Something that wouldn't require a full-scale exorcism, but it might work."

"What's that?" Nora asked.

"Holy water."

"Yes." Nora nodded. "Okay then. Let's try that."

Ally grumbled. "Would that damage the box?"

The father met her gaze. "I suppose it's possible. What are your concerns?"

"I just think... we're rushing into this. I know Blanco is sick, probably from his connection with the box, but—"

Nora's face warmed. "You still want to keep it? After all you know about it?"

"It's not what you think it is," Ally said, her voice rising. "It's just a tool. Nothing I can't handle, *if you just give me some time*."

"Is it *that* important to you, Ally?" Nora asked. "Blanco's going to die. Lucy would be destroyed without him. And where did you ever get the idea that it provides protection, anyway?"

"My research." Ally crossed her arms over her chest.

Nora shook her head. "That thing isn't protecting anyone—it's dangerous. We've seen that."

"It's a mistake to destroy it—not yet."

"Why? What's the real reason? You said it provides protection, but I just don't see it. Is it really so valuable to you?"

"You don't understand."

"Help me to understand then. Is it the mystery of what's inside of it?"

"I already know what's inside," Ally said. "It is a connection to something deeper, but it's not what you think. That box is our only defense against what's coming."

Nora narrowed her eyes. "What's coming?"

"You've already seen it." Ally gestured toward the door. "In the parking lot, in Lucy's bedroom. Gabriel unleashed something evil before he died, and this is the only way to stop it."

"You're wrong," Nora said and turned to face Father Tony. He was watching them with wide eyes. "Is she making any sense to you?"

He tilted his head in thought. "Regardless of what she believes, I think we need to take action on some level. The holy water shouldn't damage the box—no effect on it, physically—if you're concerned about preserving it. Whether the cleaning process solves the problem with Blanco remains to be seen, but we should see the effects immediately if it works."

Nora struck a somber tone. "Could it kill him?"

"It might. But if we do nothing..."

"How long will it take?" she asked him.

"The process won't take long. I can bless the water, go through the sanctification rite at the church, and be finished within an hour. I normally don't do things this... extreme, but under the circumstances..."

"Thank you, Father," Nora said. "Let's get started."

"There's got to be a different way," Ally said softly. "I'll keep it away from Blanco. I'll keep it locked up so nobody can get to it. This is wrong."

Nora turned to face her sister. "You're wrong. Let's get this done."

Father Tony stood. "I'll take Blanco in my car. Are we in agreement?"

Nora glared at Ally. "We agree."

Ally was silent for a moment, but then finally nodded.

::: center
❊ 19 ❊
:::

lly cradled the box in her arms as she followed Nora and Father Tony into St. Michael's Catholic Church. He'd slipped on a black shirt and his clerical collar before they'd left his house, explaining to them it was better not to arrive wearing his street clothes—it would attract unwanted attention.

Nora carried Blanco in his carrier at her side. He was barely moving, although his eyes were cracked open. Despite Ally's desire to protect the box from destruction, she was right. They needed to do something—if only to keep him from dying.

Squeezing the box against her chest, Ally clung to what Father Tony had promised her on the way out—that the holy water would have no effect on it physically. But would it change its ability to connect on a psychical level? The thought chilled her. They were acting recklessly, seemingly oblivious to its potential. The box wasn't evil. It was misunderstood. Couldn't they see beyond what was happening with Blanco? It was hurting him, yes—but it could help them as well. Tess had explained everything. And Nora, despite her objections, still needed it.

But it seemed she'd run out of time. Nora and Father Tony were determined to go through with it. She would just need to let them carry out their plans and take the box back to Eleanor when it was all over with to evaluate the extent of the damage.

Rushing toward the back of the sanctuary, a few parishioners glanced at them along the way, but they didn't stop. Father Tony ignored them, while Ally forced a smile.

Circling around behind the altar, they gathered in a small room filled with sacred objects. There were tall candles, ornate crosses, a row of robes hanging against one wall, and even a sink in the corner.

Nora placed Blanco's carrier on the floor, then leaned down and peered inside. "Hang in there, little guy."

Father Tony shut the door behind them and let out a breath. "We made it, although I expect I'll receive a few questions after this is over. But the sacristy should provide us with the privacy we need."

Ally set the box down on a small table and then stepped back, standing beside Nora with her arms folded over her chest.

Father Tony picked up a silver vessel and started whispering something under his breath like a prayer. He waved the vessel above the box while making the sign of a cross over his chest.

Water sprinkled down from the vessel.

Ally tensed as the drops tapped against the wood.

Father Tony flinched but didn't back away.

The air went silent for a moment as they held their breath.

Nothing happened.

Was it over? Was that it?

He continued for several seconds, chanting mixed phrases in Latin and English, while some of the water pooled in the center.

"It's not working," Ally said.

He stared down at it and then grinned. "Perhaps you've seen too many movies."

"But," Nora said, "how will we know when it's... safe?"

"I suppose an item like this is never truly safe." He stared at it for a moment, then touched the sides of the lid and opened it.

Everything was there—the parchments, Tess's notes, the statue.

Ally inched forward with her hand out. "The papers will get wet."

He nodded. "They will."

She shook her head. "I haven't translated all the words yet—their meaning and translations will be lost forever."

He glanced at Ally curiously. "Would you like to come back another time?"

"No." Nora waved dismissively at her sister. "Definitely not. Let's finish this today. Now."

Before Ally could make another objection, he splashed holy water across everything, whispering another quiet prayer.

Ally gasped in a breath.

Nothing.

After a few seconds, she exhaled.

The water had wet the papers, but the words were still clear. The ink hadn't smeared. Not yet, anyway.

Nora gestured to the vessel in Father Tony's hands. "Are you sure that stuff is...?"

He grinned. "It is blessed, I assure you. I did it myself, following church protocol. For all practical purposes, the water is a tool for sanctification, a holy instrument of God. If evil had attached itself to the object, it's gone now."

He waited for a moment, watching her response.

"But I don't see..." Nora shook her head. "I have to be sure. We have to do more."

He sighed. "I'm not sure what else I can do."

Nora pointed to the holy water. "Do you have more of that?"

He gave her a curious look. "Would you like to take some home with you?"

"Not home," she said. "But can you bless, like, a bucket of it at a time?"

His eyes widened. "I suppose it's—"

Nora gestured to the sink in the corner. "Or just fill up the sink, and we'll dunk the whole thing in there. I think it'll fit."

"Are you serious?" Ally scoffed.

"That would be unusual," Father Tony said, "but... we can use the sink, if you'd prefer."

"Perfect." Nora's face lit up.

He turned to Ally as if to get her approval. She wasn't watching them. Instead, she stared at the floor with a scowl while keeping silent. She didn't object, instead telling herself it would be over soon, and that she would never let them near the box ever again.

A moment later, Father Tony stepped over to the sink, plugged the bottom, and turned on the tap water.

"How long does it take?" Nora asked.

"For what?"

"To make the water... holy."

"Not long." The water slowly rose higher.

As the water neared the top, Ally took in a sharp breath.

"After this is completed." Father Tony shut off the water. "I suggest you leave the box with me this time. I shouldn't have doubted myself. Burying it here, within consecrated ground, is where it belongs."

Ally shook her head. "The holy water should be enough. After this is over, I'm taking the box with me."

"You say it as if the process were nothing more than erasing chalk from a chalkboard." Father Tony narrowed his eyes. "If this object truly is connected with a demon, then it might stay corrupted forever, even after dunking it in holy water. By burying it, you prevent anyone else from discovering it in the future."

"I'm sure that's unnecessary."

Nora turned to her sister again. "We shouldn't take any chances."

Ally didn't meet her sister's gaze. "This will be enough."

When the water filled the sink almost to the top, Father Tony grabbed a Bible and began the process of blessing the water. He took it all seriously, taking his time to go through everything methodically and carefully. When he was done, he stepped back and gestured to the water.

"I'll let you do the honors," he said to Nora.

Ally stepped forward instead. "I'll do it."

Nora met her gaze. "Are you sure?"

"Let's just get this over with."

Nora stepped back.

"Here we go." Ally gently placed the box in the water, and it floated on the surface for a short time until she opened the lid and submerged the whole thing with both hands.

The water rushed in, filling the box, and it sank to the bottom. The parchment, the statue, Tess's note to Gabriel—it all went down. Her sister winced, and a moment later the parchment and paper floated to the surface. They were soaked thoroughly this time, but the box and statue remained at the bottom.

A flurry of bubbles rose to the surface. Smaller ones. Then a fine mist floated off the surface like—steam.

Ally yanked her hands out of the water and jumped back. "It's... hot!" she cried. "Boiling!"

The water sizzled as more bubbles and steam sputtered into the air. The scalding water splashed across Ally's clothes.

Father Tony looked at them curiously. "It was cold coming from the faucet."

The water gurgled on its own, splashing up over Ally's arms and burning her skin. Some of the water spattered over her clothes. Ally took another step back, her eyes wide with fear.

Nora yanked on her arm. "Get away from it!"

Blanco let out a pained cry. His face was pressed against the bars of the carrier, watching them with wide eyes.

Father Tony stepped forward, pushing Ally out of the way, while blocking both of them from the water with his arm while gesturing toward the door. "Run!"

A moment later, the water exploded into the air. The basin groaned and spewed a column of liquid fire, like lava erupting from the earth's core. The burning droplets spattered over his clothes and hissed when they touched him.

At first, the father didn't seem to notice that his shirt had caught fire. He staggered, throwing an arm out to shield them from the blast.

"Father!" Ally yelled, gesturing to the line of flames crawling up his sleeve and moving across his chest.

He panicked when he saw them, slapping at the flames while charging across the room toward a fire extinguisher in the corner. Before he reached it, he ripped off his flaming black shirt and collar, and threw them to the floor, using the extinguisher to put them out. He stood bare-chested a moment later. His skin was red where the flames had touched it, and the smell of burnt cloth filled the air.

As the flames spread, the fire alarm blared. The sounds of screams and panic came through the closed door of the sacristy.

"Go!" Father Tony gestured for them to leave as he swept the extinguisher's exhaust over the sink, the walls, the floor—everything.

The flames died down, for a moment, until they seemed to take on a life of their own. The twisting flames reached up toward Father Tony like crooked fingers. Steam and smoke filled the air.

Nora grabbed Blanco's carrier and opened the door, pulling at Ally's arm, but she resisted. She refused to leave the box behind. Instead, she turned back just outside the doorway.

"Don't!" Nora cried.

Ally ignored her. The smoke cleared just enough, and she dared to peer into the sink again. Every drop of the water was gone. The box was nearly unrecognizable—warped and charred —while the parchment and Tess's handwritten notes were gone. Only the stone statue remained.

Nora and Father Tony tried to pull her back, but she resisted. Despite the smoke and heat, she reached into the sink and scooped out the statue. Gripping it with wide-eyed fascination, she cradled it in her arms with steam still drifting off its surface.

Father Tony covered himself with a white linen cloth from a table nearby while his black shirt still smoldered on the floor.

"Do you think it worked?" Ally asked him.

He met her gaze. His eyes were wide and full of shock. "I suspect... more is required."

Nora stayed by Father Tony's side as the sound of fire trucks roared in the distance. Ally was sitting nearby with her arms wrapped around the statue in her lap, her head down. She'd gone quiet after a group of firefighters and police rushed in, scrambling to assess the damage and move everyone out of the way.

Blanco had come alive after the incident, pacing in his small space and letting out a series of meows as if pleading for someone to comfort him. She wanted to hold him in her arms, but all she could do was stroke his fur through the bars. "I can't let you out, Blanco—not yet."

The scars on his flesh had started to heal. They were no longer raw and red. It seemed that whatever they had done had worked.

A small crowd had gathered outside the church, as well as in the sanctuary, their curious eyes fixed on them as if hungry for something scandalous to tell their families when they got home. Nora kept her face down.

At least the box was gone—destroyed. Problem solved.

Smoke and a toxic stench hung in the air. It would take a long time for it to clear, and even longer for Father Tony to get over the trauma, judging by the way he kept glancing back to the sink and the box in Ally's lap with wide eyes. He'd gotten burned, but not badly—only first-degree burns, according to what the EMTs had said.

The police took notes from everyone. Father Tony explained the events away as just a small accident with a candle. They seemed comfortable with that explanation after scrutinizing the sink and surrounding area.

Despite his minor injuries, Father Tony accepted a ride to the hospital in the ambulance. But before he left, he grabbed Ally's arm and spoke in a commanding tone, "I need you to destroy whatever survived—today."

"We'll take it away now." Nora nodded once. "We'll destroy it."

"How?" he asked sharply. "And *where* are you going to destroy it?"

Ally looked up and shook her head, her face full of bitterness. "Does it really matter?"

"Yes!" His brows jumped. "It definitely matters. It should be done *right*. I trusted you to take care of this before, so this time I want proof that it's gone. I underestimated its power, and I won't sleep until I know it's gone. I'm afraid I underestimated... everything."

"We'll take a hammer to it if you want," Nora said. "Smash it into pieces."

He nodded. "That should be enough. The holy water should have cleansed everything inside and severed any connections to evil, but... I need to be sure."

"I understand." Nora nodded. "What kind of proof do you need?"

"Record it on your phone and send me the video," Father Tony said.

"You want us to record it?" Ally scoffed.

"Yes," he said. "It's the least you could do after all that's happened. But get it done. Send the thing back to hell."

"We will," Nora answered.

Father Tony crouched beside Blanco's carrier and peered in at him. The cat met his gaze and let out a steady purr.

Father Tony smiled warmly. "He's already getting stronger. If you hadn't gotten to me in time…"

"We won't let you down," Nora said.

Ally nodded, while tilting her head a bit. Nora had seen her sister make that expression so many times before—she wasn't committing to anything.

Father Tony seemed to get the same impression. With the EMTs standing by, he stepped inside the sacristy again and came back with a white linen. He walked straight to Ally, held it out, and whispered, "At least, take this. I blessed it, and it will keep the item pure until you destroy it."

She accepted it but didn't wrap it around the statue right away. "Thank you."

"*But*," he emphasized, "destroy it. In all my years, I've never experienced anything like this. The statue has no place in this world."

And then he was gone, and they were standing outside the church, moving through a crowd of onlookers toward their car. They kept their faces down to avoid the expressions of those around them—so full of curiosity and pity. Ally had taken the statue with her, wrapped now in the linen as if to keep *it* safe instead of keeping *her* safe, and she clutched it against her chest like a baby.

They didn't speak until they were inside the car with Blanco in the backseat.

Nora turned to face her sister, who was staring out the window in the opposite direction, toward the church. "You should have left it there."

"What does it matter?" Ally said. "It's sanctified, right? It's just a pretty rock now."

"We have to finish what we started."

Ally narrowed her eyes and turned sharply to face her sister.

"What for? It can't hurt anyone anymore. What difference does it make now?"

"Maybe you're right," she said. "But we can't take that chance—especially after what happened in there. Father Tony might have died. I agree with what he said—we need to completely destroy it."

"I think I should keep it," she said. "I know what I'm doing, and it's got historical value."

Nora glanced down at the statue in her sister's arms. She hadn't let it out of her sight, even for a moment, since lifting it out of the sink in the church. "Is it really that important to you?"

She scoffed. "You don't understand."

"Help me understand."

"Okay, let me try," she said. "There is no good or evil in the universe. Only experiences. Some of them can seem good or bad in the moment, but they all serve a purpose. This—" She lifted the statue a few inches. "—serves a purpose for both, or it did anyway. It's a shame what happened in there. I'm sorry the father got burned. But you need to understand something—*this* is just a tool. And if we don't use the right tools to confront malicious spirits and dark forces, then they're just going to grow stronger and stronger until— You need to fight fire with fire, Nora. Flames are neither good nor bad. They just do what they do. You're trying to put them all out, while I'm trying to use them to light the way and keep us safe."

"If you play with fire, you're going to get burned." Nora smirked.

Ally looked away. "That's cute."

"You've never taken anything this far before." Nora furrowed her brow. "Where are you getting these ideas?"

Ally rolled her eyes and glanced away. "You're too worried. This is the same stuff we've surrounded ourselves with all our lives."

"No." She shook her head. "Not like this. Nothing *demonic*. How can you think that playing with this stuff is safe?"

"I spend a lot of time learning about new concepts," Ally said. "You know that. I can't help it. This stuff flows in our veins."

"But this isn't all the stuff Mom and Dad taught us—not the superficial occult world they preached for the purpose of making money. You've gone down the rabbit hole with this. You're really taking it seriously—*too* seriously."

"You're blowing this out of proportion. It's not dangerous—not like you think."

Nora scoffed. "It nearly killed Father Tony."

"But it *didn't* kill him," she said. "And all of this only happened because you two decided to dunk the thing in holy water."

"What were we supposed to do?" Nora asked.

"Just... let me handle it."

Nora shook her head and met her sister's gaze. "Who told you it's not dangerous? Wherever you're getting this information, it needs to stop. I just hope you wake up before it's too late."

Ally went silent, and Blanco let out a soft meow.

❧ 2 I ❧

When they returned home, Nora followed Ally into the parlor. Daniel stood near the back corner with a roller in his hand, smearing a fresh coat of beige paint over the drawings Lucy had made earlier that morning on the walls. The crayon lines were smudged. Had he tried to clear them off with soap and water first, and then had given up?

Ally still cradled the statue in one arm. It was wrapped in the white linen Father Tony had given her before the ambulance had carried him away.

Daniel glanced over at them when they stepped inside. He was frowning while scrutinizing the object in Ally's arms. He wiped his brow with the back of his hand but kept silent and continued painting.

Lucy burst out of the back room. She seemed to be in a panic and out of breath until she spotted Blanco's carrier at Nora's side. "There you are!"

Nora set the carrier down, and her daughter let out Blanco a moment later. Some of his fur was still stained with dried blood that Father Tony had started to clean away earlier. Both of them scurried away into the corner.

Daniel turned back toward them, sniffing the air. "What's

that smell? Like something burning." His gaze locked on the cloth in Ally's arms. "What's that?"

"Nothing important."

He frowned. "Tell me you didn't bring more of that stuff in here."

Ally pulled back, tucking the bundle closer to her side. "Since when are you worried about what I bring into my apartment?"

"What is it this time?" He narrowed his eyes. "Something connected with devil worship?"

Nora stepped between them. "It's not what you think."

"Then what is it?"

"You don't need to worry about it," she said. "We're not keeping it, anyway. We already got rid of everything you saw earlier this morning in Ally's apartment. It's gone."

He turned away from them and started painting again. "I know. I checked."

"You went snooping around my apartment when I wasn't there?" Ally's face flushed red with anger.

"I was looking for Blanco," he said. "You were gone, and I didn't know if you'd left him behind or what."

"You think we'd just abandon him like that?"

Daniel shrugged. "I wasn't sure. I just wanted to make sure he was okay."

Ally let out a sharp breath, then stormed away toward her apartment without another word. Nora followed her, rushing to catch up. As soon as they stepped inside the apartment, she closed the door behind them.

"Now he's violating my personal space," Ally said, heading toward the kitchen table with the statue.

"I'll talk with him later." Nora followed her. "We have to deal with that now."

They stopped at the table. Ally unwrapped the statue and set it down gently—right back where it had stood earlier that morning. She tossed the white cloth to the floor.

"I'm sure it's harmless now," she said. "Whatever happened at the church—whatever that was—I've never seen anything like that before, but I'm sure it's perfectly safe now. You don't need to worry."

"I do." Nora stepped closer, watching her sister brush her fingers along the edges of the statue. "We still have to destroy it, you know. We have to keep our word."

Ally shook her head. "That's not necessary anymore. Father Tony purified it in holy water—you saw what happened. There's absolutely no reason to destroy it. What's the harm in keeping it? It could be useful in helping me to understand the occult world better for business purposes. The thing belongs in a museum, not shattered into a thousand pieces. If you're worried about Daniel finding it, I promise I'll keep it stashed away some-where safe, away from Lucy."

Nora shook her head. "You've got to be kidding me. After what happened with Blanco and at the church, you still want to take that risk?"

"It's not a risk. Who would know better, you or I? I studied this stuff in college. I'm the expert here, so listen to me—this needs to be studied and preserved."

Nora scoffed. "A college degree makes you an expert? I think Father Tony is better qualified to make that decision."

Ally's lips pulled into a thin line, while she took a slow breath in through her nose. "You don't understand. Destroying it might cause more problems anyway. It might release something even worse than what happened at the church. Is that what you want?" Ally pressed her lips together. "Just one night, at least. I think I can finish my research on it by morning, and if I find anything—"

The door clicked open, and Lucy's voice broke the tension. "Can I come in?"

"Not yet," Nora said gently. "We've got some things to take care of first, then we'll help Daddy, okay?"

"He's grumpy." Lucy stepped inside, her eyes watering. "He threw away all my drawings."

Nora glanced over at the wall where Ally had taped all of Lucy's drawings. She hadn't noticed it before, but the wall was bare. All the skeletal stick figures, cryptic scribbles, and grim faces were gone. Despite its chilling depictions, Daniel shouldn't have done that. He'd made Lucy cry.

Nora spoke softly, "You can draw more. You're such a great artist."

"I don't think Daddy likes anything I draw."

Nora's heart ached. "He just wants you to try different types of drawings. Can you please help him paint the parlor for a few minutes? We'll join you in a bit."

"He told me to ask you if you needed anything."

Nora met Ally's gaze, then turned back to Lucy. "Tell Daddy we'll be out soon. Aunt Ally has one last thing to take care of."

Lucy left. As soon as the door clicked shut, Nora turned back to Ally and spoke in a firm tone, "Take the statue outside. I'll meet you there in a few minutes. Let's get this done."

Ally straightened in her chair. "We should talk about this first."

"No more talk." Nora waved her hand to the side. "We can't leave this unfinished. We need to destroy it completely, like we promised Father Tony."

"We almost burned down a church!" Ally stared down at the statue with wide eyes.

Nora followed her gaze. There were no signs on the statue's surface that anything had happened to it. No charred remnants, no marks of any kind. "That's why we can't wait. We have to finish what we started—now."

A flash of anger crossed Ally's face. She opened her mouth as if she might argue, but then closed it again, picked up the statue, and walked away. "I'll meet you out there."

When Nora arrived in the parking lot, Ally was already there. She was standing at the other end, with the statue in one hand and a hammer in the other. She'd wrapped the statue in a garbage bag. The thick plastic obscured the details, but its outline was still visible even from that distance.

Nora stepped toward her and called out, "Are you ready?"

Ally frowned. "Let's just get it over with."

Nora carried the empty garbage bag over to her sister and laid it out over the asphalt. It would make it easier to clean up any stray pieces of the statue after they were done. The breeze caught the edges, so she held it in place until Ally kneeled onto it and dropped the hammer at her side. The piercing clank of the hammer's metal head hitting the asphalt caught Nora off guard. She shivered. The horrific memory of what had happened at the church that morning was still too fresh in her mind. They exchanged a quick glance before Ally continued, placing the wrapped statue in the center of the bag.

Nora took out her phone, ready to record the event, and stepped back. "You'll feel better after it's gone. We both will."

Ally shook her head. "It's unnecessary."

"Let it go, Ally. It's the only way to finish this. A week from now, you'll barely remember ever owning it."

Picking up the hammer, Ally stared at the bulging section of the bag for a long moment. "What a shame. What a shame."

"It's better this way." Nora nodded once.

"Better for who? Whatever power it held before, it's gone. We saw what happened when we dunked everything in holy water. What more could he possibly want?"

"It's not *completely* gone, and after what I saw there, I'm even more sure we're doing the right thing now."

Ally grumbled a few words under her breath, then said, "Start the recording. Let's get this over with."

Nora started the video, moving close enough to clearly see the statue bulging within the bag and the hammer that Ally had lifted over her head. Ally swung it down, and it crashed against the stone with a loud crack. The sound echoed off the walls of the buildings like a gunshot. The object split in half, creating two large sections in the bag. Ally winced again and struck the remaining pieces repeatedly—over and over with rising intensity—until the thing was almost flat.

She frowned and dropped the hammer. "Is this good enough? Does this make you happy?"

Nora swallowed. The last thing she wanted was to see her sister so broken, so hopeless as she hunched over the flattened bag. Her sister even pushed her fingers through the debris as if to make her point that it was irretrievably gone.

"It's in a thousand pieces now, just like you wanted." Ally scowled. "Are you happy?"

Nora nodded. "I'm sure that wasn't easy for you. I'm proud of you."

Her sister stood there, squeezing the bag into a ball while leaving the hammer and bag behind. She turned back toward the side door, but instead of going inside, she stepped forward and opened the bag just enough so Nora could see inside.

"You'd better record what's left," she said. "So he doesn't have any doubts."

Nora nodded and aimed her phone into the bag. The debris was there at the bottom. Not a single shard was larger than a pebble. "It's over."

"I'll save what's left in case he wants me to dump it into the lake or bury it on sacred ground or something."

"Good idea." Nora nodded and paused to send the video to Father Tony, along with a short message.

We destroyed it, she wrote.

At the same time, an unseasonably chilly wind picked up again. Nora stepped forward and embraced her sister. Ally didn't resist. She even leaned into her, burying her face in Nora's shoulder. When Ally let go, Nora stepped back and gave a half-laugh.

"You were always the brave one," Nora said.

"Not as brave as you think." Ally met her gaze with watery eyes. "We'd better get inside. Daniel needs our help."

"We had to do it this way," Nora said. "We had no choice."

"We won't mention it ever again."

Nora nodded as her sister turned away and trudged inside carrying the remains of the statue.

It was finally over. The sense of closure swept through her. Whatever had harmed Blanco was gone, and hopefully, along with it, the last remnant of anything connected to Gabriel.

When she turned back toward the parlor, Lucy's bright face was peering out at them from the apartment window. Her little eyes were wide. Had she watched the whole thing? If she had, then she must have questions after seeing them smash a wrapped object while recording it. Hopefully, on some level, her daughter understood that this was just the way things were in their family —a little strange. It had always been that way and would always be.

Stepping inside, Lucy rushed over to them.

"What were you doing out there?" she asked. "What did you smash?"

Nora swept past her toward the parlor, but she needed to give Lucy an explanation, if only to keep her from asking again in front of Daniel. "Sometimes you need to break with the past to move forward."

"Were you breaking the statue?" Lucy asked.

"Yes," Nora said. "Please don't ask me about it ever again."

"Why not?"

"It wasn't... healthy."

"Is that what made Blanco sick? Did he try to eat it?"

"I don't think he tried to eat it," Nora said, "but it's gone now. It won't ever hurt anyone again."

23

Ally hesitated before heading out into the parking lot with the statue. As soon as her sister walked away, she turned back. She wouldn't go through with it. No way. It wasn't right. The thing was historic—priceless—and there was no way in hell she would smash it into oblivion just to appease Father Tony's groundless fear.

What was the point anyway? Father Tony had cleansed it completely and thoroughly. Whatever connection it had with the occult was gone, and it was heartbreaking to think nobody would ever get the chance to appreciate its power ever again. If only Nora knew how important it was—their best defense against whatever Gabriel had brought into this world.

She couldn't go through with Father Tony's request.

She wouldn't keep her promise.

Sorry, Father Tony.

Not yet anyway.

Cradling it against her chest through the apartment, she paused near the back door with her mind reeling. They just didn't understand its significance. Destroying it now seemed... impossible.

Nora would be waiting for her soon. She needed to get

outside with the statue, but she couldn't quite make herself step out the door.

They wanted proof, that's all—proof of its destruction. So how could she make that happen without actually destroying it?

Old props and souvenirs that her father had gathered over the years stuffed the shelves near the back door. A macabre display of occult items he'd never bothered to understand, items he'd intended to provide to Nora for her séances. But now they held no purpose. Eventually, all of them would get thrown out. None of them were authentic—not one—not like the statue. All of it was just a pile of worthless items. So what was keeping her from smashing one of *those* instead?

One of them stood out among the others. A kitschy guardian gargoyle statue her father had probably picked up at a novelty store. It bore *some* resemblance to the demon stone in her hands, with its hunched posture and imposing stare. The dimensions were almost identical, and it was roughly the same color and texture, although not quite the same. It was probably made of plaster and almost certainly hollow. The weight would be different, but Nora would never hold it.

Close enough. They'll never know the difference.

Ally picked it off the shelf and compared them side-by-side. Her father's statue weighed half as much, but it would work just fine. If she got caught, she would have to apologize. It would create a rift between them, and Nora would be furious, but it was worth the risk. She wouldn't get caught, anyway. It would be a simple matter to swap them—an illusion.

What was that old saying? It was easier to ask forgiveness than to get permission.

She lifted the statue out of the garbage bag and placed it behind the other items on the shelf. It blended in with the other items perfectly.

Nobody will ever know.

After slipping her father's statue into the bag, she took a step toward the door but stopped.

She'd forgotten the hammer.

Turning back, she dug into the closet again and found it on the floor inside her father's rusted toolbox. Its weight felt good in her hands. Smashing something in that moment might actually feel good. Maybe even cathartic. Dealing with it this way wasn't the ideal solution, but the deception was necessary to protect her sister's family. She couldn't blame them for forcing her to go through with it. It's just that they didn't understand the stakes like she did.

Stepping out into the parking lot, her heart raced. Nora wasn't there yet. Walking to the back of the parking lot, she pushed away her grin and frowned instead. She had to play the part, put on a good performance for her sister and Father Tony, and give them what they wanted. It would only take a few minutes, and she would never bring it up again.

Only a moment later, Nora stepped out of the parlor's side door and walked toward her carrying an empty garbage bag.

"Are you ready?" Nora called out.

"Let's just get it over with." Ally forced a frown. At least, she could take refuge in knowing the real statue was safely stashed away in her apartment, waiting for her when she returned.

After this was over, she had to find out if it still held any power after what Father Tony had done to it. Maybe Father Tony had permanently damaged the statue, but she had to know for certain. She had to take it back to the only person who could answer that question: the woman who had owned the statue in the first place—Tess.

24

Ally stepped up to Tess's door and knocked. The sound of a violin pierced the air, coming from somewhere inside, near the back of the house.

The woman answered a moment later, opening the door with a bright smile. "What a pleasant surprise."

Ally shook her head. "I'm afraid I've made a terrible mistake."

Tess's eyes widened and her smile faded. "Oh?"

Ally caught herself glancing back toward her car. They were far from prying eyes, shrouded by massive oak trees, but taking the statue out in the open unnerved her, after what she'd gone through to save it from destruction. She lifted it from her purse and unwrapped it in front of Tess.

Tess stared at the statue until her smile returned, and she pulled the door open. "Come in."

Ally stepped inside, and Tess closed the door behind them.

The sound of the violin grew louder, and Ally turned her head toward it. The notes wavered, but there was a raw sincerity in the music. "Someone practicing?"

Tess smiled as they started walking forward. "Eve works at it every day. I'm so proud of her, though I'm afraid she struggles to hold the instrument for any length of time because of her injuries."

Ally's heart ached at the thought of Eve struggling with anything. "I'm sorry to hear that."

"She never gives up. That's the important thing." Tess stopped and turned to face her. "Now, let's talk about your *mistake*."

"I'm not sure if I damaged it."

Tess's gaze dropped to the statue again with a curious look. "Why do you feel it's damaged?"

Ally ran her fingers across the statue's face and torso. It didn't *feel* the same—something had dulled its bristling energy—but at least nothing was broken. "My sister forced me to hand over everything to a priest. He dunked everything in holy water after she demanded that we destroy it."

Tess lost her smile. "That is unfortunate. Why did your sister feel she needed to do something so drastic?"

"It's difficult to explain," she said. "It was affecting our cat, Blanco. His scars were reacting to it strangely—like they were on fire around it. Blanco was rescued from Gabriel's home."

Tess nodded. "The white cat."

"That's him. We had to do something. We were afraid he might die from the inflammation. She forced me to take the items to the priest to have it cleansed in holy water. Unfortunately, I'm afraid I destroyed the only path to protect Nora's family. It wasn't my choice. But I think the priest stripped away all of its power."

"Poor Blanco! I remember seeing him during one of my visits with Gabriel. A lovely cat. But why are you so sure that you've permanently damaged the statue?" Tess held a curious grin. "It doesn't work that way."

A wave of relief swept through Ally. "Oh, thank God."

"It's not surprising that Nora made you get rid of it. She's a pragmatic one, isn't she?"

"She can be," Ally said. "They wanted to destroy it

completely, smash it into pieces, but I saved it at the last minute."

"Who are *they*?"

"Nora and... Father Tony, Gabriel's neighbor, the one who gave me the statue."

Tess nodded and led Ally toward the living room. "I see. And how did he acquire it?"

"I think he's a friend of Gabriel's family. They asked him to help dispose of the more unsavory items—objects associated with the occult—knowing Father Tony's background with the church."

The woman pushed aside some pillows on the couch and sat down, gesturing to Ally to take a seat at the other end.

"I know the man." Ally sat and placed the statue on the coffee table in front of them. Its dead gaze stared back at them. "A priest at St. Michael's Catholic Church, if I remember correctly."

"That's him."

She turned her attention back to the statue, staring at it with what looked like admiration. "Why on earth would anyone try to destroy such a thing? It's a beautiful work of art, crafted from rare stone. It was wise to keep it safe. Your sister doesn't understand what could've happened if she had truly broken the bond —if the seal had ruptured after all this time. Especially after... what the priest did."

"I think it worked," Ally said, not sure if she believed it herself. "The water boiled. It even set his clothes on fire."

The woman's eyes widened. "I hope he wasn't hurt."

Ally tilted her head. "Nothing serious."

"That's good." Tess softened her voice while leaning forward. "You got a taste of its power. But not its full potential. That was only a glimpse of what it can do—a fraction of the fire it once held. And your sister—did she see what happened?"

Ally nodded. "But she looked more relieved than anything after the priest was done."

"She should be terrified," Tess whispered. "It could have been much worse. The statue is a conduit to the darker realms. At least you still have it in your possession. You can still use it again to finish what you started."

"It's not damaged?" Ally asked.

"Not enough to destroy it," Tess said. "The connection is still there, although the priest weakened it. Despite his rites of purification, it can't be unbound from this world so easily. Its roots run deeper than his faith. This object was forged in a different kind of fire—ancient, divine. The kind that scars, but also protects."

"I appreciate all your help," Ally said. "I know you were only trying to make things right after what Gabriel did, but I came here to give it back. Before my sister finds it. Before Blanco gets near it again."

Tess smiled politely. "You should do what you feel is right, but the scar's reaction to the statue will fade in time. The cat will survive. What matters now is that the statue still holds power. It can safely protect your home, your sister's family, just as I said before. Nothing has changed. There's still time to use it."

"What *exactly* is it protecting us from? My sister is having nightmares, along with Lucy, but does the entity attacking us have a name? If it's not the helper demon Ezeran, then is it Moloch?"

Tess shook her head. "Not Moloch. His presence would shake the world, but there are lesser demons who might have slipped through."

"Like who?"

"It's hard to tell." Tess leaned back. "Gabriel didn't just open a door. He made a pact with Moloch that allowed something malevolent to enter this realm, something that hasn't yet found a form."

"Do you know what it is?"

"I know it's hungry." Tess paused with a distant stare. "And I know it hasn't stopped looking—"

A cough came from the hallway.

Ally turned sharply in her seat.

Tess's daughter Eve moved toward them in her wheelchair and stopped at the edge of her sight. The girl stared at Ally without blinking. Her lips were bluish in the soft light, her breathing shallow but rhythmic. A violin and bow sat in her lap.

"She wanted to say hello." Tess gazed lovingly at her daughter's face. "Didn't you, sweetheart?"

Eve didn't move. She just stared, playing with the strands of her hair, pulling it down over her eyes as if trying to hide herself from them.

"She needs to work on her manners, I know," Tess said.

"She's fine." Ally smiled. "Should I come back another time?"

"Not at all," Tess said. "She was just in the back helping me to restore some antiques. It's one of the few things she enjoys doing anymore."

The girl's face was sunken, hunched forward a bit with a waxy complexion. Her hands were dirty—the color of rust. She looked thinner than the last time Ally had stopped by.

"I'm not sure how much longer I can take her antique hunting with me." Anguish spread across Tess's face. "I have arthritis in my knees, and it's getting more difficult to get around. But she's very attached to our work. We're quite a team."

"That's the way it was with me and Nora... until recently."

"I'm happy to assist you in any way I can."

"That's the thing." Ally glanced down at the statue. "Nora wants me to stay away from this. From all of it."

Tess grinned. "But you won't, will you? You've already seen what lies behind the veil. You've touched something most people spend their whole lives chasing. It's impossible to go back, Ally. You're not meant to."

"I just want it to stop." Ally squeezed the statue. "The nightmares. The strange drawings. Lucy's been drawing things she can't possibly understand, and Nora and Daniel both blame me. It's causing a lot of friction between us."

"The child is open," Tess said. "The way some children are. She's sensitive to things unseen. She attracts it."

"You think she's a target?"

"I think she's vulnerable." Tess narrowed her eyes a bit. "That's why she needs protection. Real protection. And the statue is the key. But it must be placed near the thinnest part of the veil."

"In Nora's house?"

Tess tilted her head. "As close to the target as possible."

Ally swallowed. "I don't know if I can do that, after what happened to Blanco."

"You must," Tess whispered. "The girl's nightmares will pass. But the danger—if unguarded—will not."

"If Lucy is the target," Ally said, "then... why? What do they want from her?"

"It's hard to say," Tess straightened in her seat. "Some malicious spirits simply delight in tormenting the living, and some of them won't stop until they're satisfied."

"But how does someone satisfy a demon?"

Tess glanced away. "Death, I'm afraid."

Silence filled the air for a moment.

"So, why *her*?" Ally asked. "Why not someone else?"

"My guess is the entity simply followed Gabriel's spirit to your sister's house after he allowed them to enter this world. Gabriel went there to torment your sister—for revenge—but he also brought with him the evil he'd unleashed. He's gone, but they remain."

Behind her, Eve let out a sudden, high-pitched hum—off-key, rhythmic, almost childlike. Her fingers tapped against her armrest, out of sync with her breath.

After Tess didn't seem to notice, Ally glanced over at the girl and met her gaze. "Is she all right?"

"She's always watching," Tess said, still not looking back. "She sees more than I can. That's why we're so close."

Tess slid closer, leaned forward and touched Ally's hands. "We'll do a short meditation now. It will help quiet the noise in your mind."

Ally nodded reluctantly.

"Don't be afraid." Tess stood, stepping across the room and lighting a few candles on a bookshelf. Within seconds, the smell of incense filled the air. "All we're doing is opening the mind. Letting a little light in."

"I'm not afraid," Ally said.

"That's clear." The woman returned to the couch and sat closer this time with a straightened posture. "Breathe in... now out. Let go of the noise, the thoughts. Let go of yourself."

But the moment Ally closed her eyes, the sound of Eve's wheelchair creaked closer.

Darkness swept in around them as she focused on each breath. Her body felt weightless within seconds, as if sinking slowly through the floor.

"Ally," Tess whispered again. "What are you feeling?"

She couldn't open her eyes now, even if she tried. "I'm floating."

"Where are you?"

The darkness swept away, and she wasn't in Tess's house anymore. She wasn't anywhere she recognized, standing ankle-deep in a field of ash. It was simmering hot with no signs of a fire. Steam rose from the ground as a soft wind carried the voices of children in the distance. They were crying, chanting, screaming.

Ahead of her, two stone pillars stood like monuments to a Roman god, with symbols carved into the sides she recognized from Gabriel's notes. There were the same designs showing an open flame, spirals, jagged lines, and things she didn't understand. Between the two stone pillars stood a massive throne made from what looked like human bones and black obsidian stone. Someone wearing a black cloak sat in it, with smoke rising around them like a veil.

She couldn't see their face, just two points of red light glowing from somewhere where its eyes should be. Horns rose from its head. It looked up at her and met her gaze.

It *saw* her. It knew she was there, and a chill ran up her spine.

But something even more chilling caught her attention. A child stood at its feet with their arms raised to the figure in surrender.

This was the scene Lucy had drawn on paper and on the parlor wall. The little girl's imagination brought to life in her mind's eye. Had Lucy had the same vision?

"What do you see?" Tess asked.

"A demon," Ally whispered.

"What does he look like?"

Ally described them in all of its horrifying detail this time.

"Yes," Tess said when Ally was done. "That is Ezeran, the helper."

Within the darkness of Ally's vision, the girl turned around, and Ally's stomach churned.

Lucy.

The demon hovered over the girl, with thick darkness surrounding them. Lucy stood glowing with golden light. Her form radiated even as a hoard of dark figures beckoned to them from all sides.

"Aunt Ally," Lucy said in a soft voice. "You don't have to be afraid. He won't hurt us."

Ally stepped toward Lucy, reaching toward her niece, ready to yank her away at the first sign of distress. The tension pulled at every muscle in Ally's body.

How could Lucy possibly be safe in the presence of that... thing?

"He's not a thing, silly!" Lucy glanced up at the imposing dark presence above them. "He's my friend."

Ally shook her head, but Lucy's little face beamed with delight and peace.

"He promised me he wouldn't hurt me." Lucy gestured toward the seething figures twisting and contorting within the darkness around them. None of them were moving forward, seemingly held back by the power of the figure on the throne. Despite Ally's fears, it *was* working.

Ally glanced up at Ezeran again. His gaze was cold, but he made no motion to harm either of them.

"You see?" Lucy said. "I'm perfectly safe here, Aunt Ally!"

Ally nervously nodded. She stepped toward Lucy, but instead of reaching the girl, Ally was yanked upward. Her body shuddered as an icy chill flashed through every muscle. When she opened her eyes, she was still shaking from the vision. It took her a moment to ground herself again. She was back in Tess's house, sitting in the same spot, with Tess staring at her with a knowing grin.

"Do you see the truth now?" Tess asked.

"I... saw him," Ally said. "Ezeran... and Lucy."

"Good," Tess whispered. "You know what to do. You must fight fire with fire. It's the only way."

"What should I do now?" Ally asked. "To protect them?"

"I will write out the instructions." Tess stood with a bit of difficulty. "It's not too difficult, but you must perform them *exactly* as I write it. Gabriel diverged from my instructions, took a different path, and we know where that landed him. The statue only needs to be in the girl's room for a couple of hours during the night. That alone will be enough to deflect any dark entities."

"Nothing more?"

Tess shook her head. "Just one night, while she sleeps. Can you abide by my rules?"

"I can."

$\maltese$ 25 $\maltese$

Nora sat at the kitchen table beside Lucy, comforting her as Daniel rushed through the house, checking all the windows for leaks. He was pulling up all the blinds, running his fingers along every windowsill.

She'd made a cup of hot cocoa, if only to calm her nerves as the storm had grown louder. Lucy was drawing again with crayons—swirls and symbols that echoed the drawings she'd done in Ally's apartment. They were clearly occult in nature, although Daniel hadn't seemed to notice them yet, or at least he wasn't saying anything. The colors she'd chosen were limited to dark hues mixed with bright orange and red.

Nora hadn't said anything about the drawing until now. "Sweetheart, what are you making this time?"

"It's just something I saw," Lucy said.

"From your imagination?"

Lucy shook her head. "Something from Ally's apartment."

Nora swallowed, leaning in toward her daughter. At least Daniel wasn't in the room to hear that. She lowered her voice. "Maybe you should draw something else for a while. Something beautiful. Can you do that? Maybe you saw something on TV or in the kitten video we watched earlier."

Lucy stared back with wide, innocent eyes. "Yes, Mommy. I'm sorry."

"No need to apologize, honey. I understand you've seen a lot of scary things lately."

"They're not all scary." Lucy stared down at her drawing again. "They're just things I saw, and I want to remember them."

When Lucy started on another one with the same colors, Nora pulled it away. "Let's try something different tonight, okay? Can you draw something for Daddy? Maybe something special just for him?"

"Like what?"

"Maybe a car or a mountain. You know Daddy likes to go hiking and climbing once in a while."

"But I've never seen a mountain in real life," she said.

"You've never seen any of this in real life either, though, right?"

Lucy shrugged.

"You haven't, have you?"

"Not really."

"Well," Nora said, "let's just use our imagination, okay?"

"Okay."

The girl didn't seem thrilled at Nora's direction but started on a fresh page just as Daniel returned to the kitchen and stood over Lucy, watching her draw for a moment before saying anything to either of them. Just as she had finished drawing what looked like a church steeple and jagged lines, Daniel leaned down further and pushed up beside her.

"What are you drawing?" he asked softly.

"It's a mountain," she said. "It's for you."

Daniel's expression changed. His eyes widened, and he glanced at Nora with a growing smile. "I like that a lot better. Let's just keep moving in that direction."

He walked over to the refrigerator, pulled out a beer, and sat at the table with them. He took a few sips before speaking again.

"Speaking of churches," he said to Nora. "Are you going to

tell me why you and Ally stopped by again to see that priest today? Anything I should know?"

Nora shook her head. "Not much to tell. I just needed a little clarity."

"Clarity about what?"

"Everything we've experienced lately."

He nodded as if he understood. "You think that priest can help?"

She knew what he meant. Help Ally. Help Lucy. Help her steer away from their growing fascination with the occult.

"It's not just her," Nora said. "Things haven't been exactly normal lately. My nightmare. What happened under Lucy's bed."

Lucy glanced up and then back down again.

"You've got to get away from it somehow," Daniel said. "You can't embrace that stuff and expect to sleep well at night. It pollutes your mind."

"It never bothered me before," she said. "In all the years my family ran their business, I never had any trouble sleeping."

He shrugged and leaned into her while wrapping his arm around her waist. "I just worry about you."

The rain battered the windows in waves, and the wind seemed to shake the house. Lightning flashed, and a few seconds later a crack of thunder roared through the house.

"Mommy, I'm scared." Lucy glanced under the table. "Where's Blanco?"

Before anyone could answer, Lucy jumped out of her chair and scrambled around the kitchen until she found the cat in the corner. Carrying him back to the table, she held him close to her chest and stroked his fur.

"It's just a storm," Nora said. "Nothing to be afraid of. We're all together."

Another flash of lightning burst through the windows that Daniel had uncovered to look for leaks. It lit up the living room, but also something just outside the window. A dark silhouette moving within the shadows. It had slipped out of view just as she'd focused on it, and the hairs on the back of her neck bristled.

Turning her attention back to the table, she folded Lucy's earlier drawings in half so Daniel wouldn't see them.

"Lucy," she said gently, "get ready for bed now. Take Blanco with you."

Lucy glanced back toward the open, uncovered windows. "Can I sleep with you?"

Nora shook her head. "Not tonight, honey. You're getting too old to sleep in our bed anymore. And you have Blanco in your room, remember?"

The cat's ears twitched. But instead of looking toward them, the fur along his back straightened, and he stared toward the living room—toward the same spot Nora had focused on moments earlier. She followed his gaze and saw nothing, except he didn't look away.

What do you see, little guy?

She searched the darkness a little longer, then turned back to Lucy. "Time for bed. We've had enough excitement today."

Lucy grabbed her drawing of the mountaintop that she had started, and instead of finishing it, she drew a heart and her name at the bottom before handing it to Daniel. "I drew this for you, Daddy."

He looked it over and then kissed her forehead. "This is what I like. Draw more awesome pictures like this."

"I will," she said.

Lucy rushed away with Blanco in her arms, keeping her head low and not glancing around. As soon as she was gone, Daniel turned to Nora.

"What are we going to do about Ally?"

"What about her?" she asked.

"Is that why you went to the church? To get the priest to straighten her out?"

"Daniel," Nora said firmly. "Ally doesn't need to be straightened out. She's just a little... independent."

"I'm fine with that." He finished his beer and crushed the can in his hand. "She can do whatever she wants, but I'm just afraid she might try to steer you back toward how things used to be."

"She won't." Nora took another sip of her hot cocoa.

He stood up. "You coming to bed?"

She shook her head. "Too much on my mind. I'll be in there shortly."

His face was full of concern. "I wasn't very patient with Ally today."

"No," Nora said, "you weren't. She's only trying to do the right thing. But I understand. She gets under my skin sometimes too."

"I'll try... to be more open-minded. I'm trying to do the right thing too."

Nora nodded. "I know."

He stood and hovered beside her silently for a moment before walking away.

Finishing her hot cocoa, she waited until Daniel had gone upstairs before she stood. The uncovered window in the living room caught her attention again. It was impossible to ignore. She didn't dare to look straight at it, but from the corner of her eye she could see something moving just beyond the glass.

Tree branches?

The driving wind pressed against the glass. Something dark and crooked filled the window's darkness. Not trees. It had a different shape. Something darker than the shadows around it, and it swayed back and forth. She avoided staring at it directly, but was it trying to get her attention? A chill ran up her spine.

My mind is tired.

My eyes are tired.

Yes, that's all there was to it. She was exhausted and... It happened to everyone, the momentary blurs, visual static from tired eyes. The technical term was peripheral drift illusion. She'd heard the term used by ghost skeptics many times over the years, along with pareidolia—the brain misinterpreting random stimuli into something meaningful. Most sightings could be explained by one of the two.

Most.

But she couldn't shake the feeling that someone was watching her.

Lightning flashed twice, followed by two thunderous booms. The house shook with each one.

That must have scared Lucy.

She imagined her daughter clinging to Blanco. Nora would need to check on her soon, sit beside her probably until she fell asleep. It wasn't just for Lucy's comfort but for her own too.

Another flash followed by a crack seconds later. The storm intensified. How would any of them sleep that night?

Another crack filled the air.

Nora nearly dropped her empty cup of cocoa on the way to the sink. With trembling hands, she managed to set it down without breaking it and stepped toward the stairs. The rafters creaked in the torrential wind and rain.

Lucy screamed.

26

Nora raced up the stairs. Daniel met her in her hallway, just outside Lucy's door, having charged out of their bedroom at the same time. They looked at each other for a moment before they both rushed into Lucy's bedroom together.

They found their daughter standing beside her bed, staring with wide eyes at the window. She pointed at it frantically. "Someone was standing out there."

Daniel ran over to the window and looked outside in both directions, pushing aside the blinds without using the cord.

Nora pulled Lucy in against her side. "Maybe it was just some birds trying to get out of the storm."

Lucy shook her head. "Not a bird, Mommy. I saw a man."

"Are you sure?" Daniel checked the window locks and then let the blinds drop. "Nobody could have climbed up there in this weather. You probably saw the tree branches or some birds, like Mommy said."

Another flash of lightning and a crack of thunder filled the air. Lucy trembled in Nora's arms. Then another crack without any lightning. But this sound didn't come from outside. It came from downstairs. It was sharp and familiar, like someone had slammed their front door shut.

They all froze.

"Didn't you lock the door?" Nora asked him.

"Of course I did." He rushed out of the room before Nora could say anything else.

Nora turned Lucy away from the window and nudged her forward to the edge of the bed. Blanco came up and pushed in alongside them. He was also wide-eyed and kept glancing back toward the window, staring at it as if whatever had frightened Lucy would return.

"What is it, Mommy?" Lucy asked. "Is it that bad man again?"

"No, honey," Nora said. "It's not Gabriel. He's gone. Forever."

Daniel returned a moment later but continued past Lucy's open bedroom door toward the stairs. He was holding a pistol out in front of him with a stern gaze.

"Is Daddy going to shoot someone?" Lucy's eyes widened with fear.

Nora swallowed. "I hope not."

Lucy's bedroom door shifted slightly. The air pressure in the house had changed. Had someone opened a window or the front door again?

Something else crashed downstairs. It wasn't the door this time. A flurry of crashing noises filled the air.

Daniel was down there.

She imagined him engaged in a struggle, and the thought sent her heart racing. She scanned Lucy's room. There had to be something there should could use as a weapon. A small lamp, a child's umbrella, a pair of scissors. Nothing useful.

Were they overreacting? The wind could have pushed the door open if they hadn't latched it properly, but that seemed unlikely. Someone *had* gotten inside. Or they had already been inside earlier and had just now escaped.

"I've got a weapon," Daniel called down the stairwell in a low, booming voice, "and I'm not afraid to use it."

The noises erupted again, a little louder this time. Furniture scraped violently across the floor, followed by the crash of wood and glass against the wall. The lights flickered and dimmed.

Someone was down there.

"I'm scared, Mommy," Lucy whispered.

"We're safe up here," Nora lied. They had to call the police. She touched her pocket, but...

Where the hell was her phone?

Daniel stomped down the stairs now, making his presence clear.

Nora stood and glanced around. Daniel had a gun, but there were plenty of knives downstairs in the kitchen. She grabbed the scissors from Lucy's dresser and held them off to the side, but Lucy still caught sight of them and started to cry.

"Are you going to kill someone, Mommy?"

Nora shook her head. "No, honey. I just want to scare them away."

"Who is it?" Lucy asked through her tears.

"I don't know." Nora glanced around. "But we should hide."

She stepped to the open bedroom door and held her breath. The house fell silent for a moment. The only sounds came from the wind rattling Lucy's bedroom window frame.

Carefully closing the bedroom door, she turned back with her pulse pounding in her ears. She led Lucy and Blanco to the closet, then squeezed them inside. Pushing aside some clothes to make more room for herself, she stepped in behind them and closed the door.

If the intruder managed to get past Daniel...

She forced herself not to finish the thought.

Her mind jumped back to what they had done at the church —the fire that had almost taken Father Tony's life, and the statue that had somehow survived. They had smashed the statue, even though Ally had warned that it might release something even worse if they did. Had she been right? Was this connected with what they'd done? It seemed unthinkable after all they'd been through. And now, this was the price of their recklessness.

Lucy was trembling in the closet with a pair of scissors in her hand. Daniel was downstairs fending off an intruder with a pistol. Their lives were on the line.

The noises erupted again downstairs, and something thumped against the ceiling directly below them as if they knew exactly where they were hiding.

Lucy cried, and the tears soaked into Nora's shirt.

It was impossible to shield her daughter from the noise. The sounds grew louder, and they were coming from everywhere.

She had to find her phone. Had she left it in her bedroom? Or downstairs?

Before she had a chance to remember, someone's voice echoed from up the stairway. Not Daniel's voice. It was something darker. A low snarling sound, like a starving animal. It wasn't human. The walls rumbled from the thunder and then the sounds of a struggle.

Then came the gunshots. Three shots rang out.

BAM BAM BAM.

Nora shuddered at each of them. She squeezed her eyes shut on the third one. Lucy pushed in against her and clutched Nora's waist.

Then silence... except for the storm battering against their house.

She had shut the bedroom door—but had she locked it? She couldn't remember.

If the intruder could get inside the house, they could certainly get through a bedroom door.

Someone was walking up the stairs.

Not Daniel—judging by the weight, the pause between each step. It was someone larger. Someone was letting out a heavy breath after each step, with the air pushing through their throat like a grumble. The wooden floors squeaked as they moved through the hallway toward them.

Where was Daniel?

Nora held back a rising panic.

How had they gotten past him?

Hadn't he shot them? Or had the gunshots come from the intruder's weapon?

Doors creaked open and slammed shut. The laundry room. The bathroom. The closet.

And then Lucy's bedroom.

But the door didn't open.

Instead, it creaked and groaned under the weight of something pushing from the outside. Cloth or fur or flesh pressing against the wood again and again as if testing it for weakness. The frame cracked but held. The doorknob jiggled.

Nora waited for it to break through.

They had to know someone was hiding from them in the bedroom. What was stopping them from stepping inside to finish them off?

Nora calculated how far they were from the window. How many seconds it would take to open it and push Lucy out onto the roof, giving her one last chance to get to safety—or even just to crouch outside on the shingles and scream for help.

She calculated her footsteps. It would take her three steps—that's all—to get over there. It would take a few seconds to get out of the closet, and another few to open the window. Ten seconds in all... if nothing went wrong.

Lucy trembled against her waist, shifting backwards within the cramped space.

Clutching the scissors in her hand, Nora calculated where she might strike the intruder first. The face? The chest? The crotch? She'd heard the first blow was the most important. She would hit it hard to give Lucy the best chance of escape.

Should she take offensive action and strike first, before the intruder got inside? Or was it better to stay hidden in the closet?

She went back and forth in her mind.

The nightmare was playing out in crisp, chilling reality. This was everything she feared for her family—a true nightmare come to life.

Her heart sank as Blanco started scratching at the door as if demanding to be let out.

She couldn't let him out. Or calm him down. None of them could leave that cramped space until she knew it was safe.

And then, the pounding.

Over and over—louder and louder—against the door, against the walls, against the floor. It came from everywhere.

Whatever it was—it wanted in.

But then—silence.

The sounds stopped.

The silence continued for several minutes. She hadn't heard anything leave the area. No sounds of footsteps going down the stairs. Was it waiting for them just outside the door?

Pressing her fingers against the closet door, she turned the handle slowly until the latch clicked open. She peeked out and caught sight of Lucy's bedroom door. Through the crack of light coming in through the bottom of her door, there was nothing on the other side. Nothing blocked the light from that angle, anyway.

She held up the scissors and turned back to Lucy, nudging her back. "Stay here," she whispered.

Lucy moaned softly but obeyed. She held Blanco in her arms until Nora had closed the closet door again, then crept toward the bedroom door.

Still no sounds from downstairs.

Where was Daniel?

Her mind imagined the worst, but she pushed it away. She wanted to run down there, call his name, and help him, but she restrained herself. She couldn't leave Lucy alone.

But after a few minutes, he still hadn't come back.

If he were okay, he would have come back, or at least called out to them.

She swallowed a scream, raised the scissors, and opened the bedroom door.

The front door slammed shut again. And the air pressure changed again—back to normal.

Still, she didn't let out her breath, but it slipped out in stuttering bursts while focusing on the silence around her. The wind rattled the window frames. And the thunder continued. Lightning flashed again, then more thunder.

She waited like that for several minutes until she couldn't take it anymore.

"Daniel?" she screamed.

Silence.

Glancing back at Lucy's bedroom door, the full extent of the damage became clear. They had almost gotten through. The entire frame was cracked and bowed inward as if someone had pushed all their weight on it. Not only from the middle, but all the way from top to bottom.

"Daniel?" she cried louder.

Silence again.

She rushed to her bedroom and spotted her phone on the dresser. Grabbing it while still extending the scissors into the darkness around her, she dialed 911.

She didn't wait for the dispatcher to answer before making her way down the stairs, calling out to Lucy to stay in her room.

"Daniel?" she called out again and continued down the stairs.

The damage was worse than she'd imagined. Someone had torn up the floors and walls, leaving behind deep gouges. Had an animal broken inside and clawed its way out? Or had someone intentionally sliced through everything with knives? A toxic smell hung in the air. An odd, familiar smell of smoke, like something from a recent nightmare. Her stomach churned.

She provided their address to the 911 dispatcher, along with a brief description of what had happened. They assured her that help was on the way and told her to stay on the line.

"Daniel?" she called out again at the bottom of the stairs.

No answer.

Their house was destroyed. The intruder had left nothing

unturned. Every piece of furniture was a mangled remnant of what it used to be. Something had blackened the walls. They almost looked scorched. Had a fire swept through? Glass lay scattered in every direction. Everything lay in a heap on the floor.

Daniel wasn't among the debris.

Rushing through it, she finally found him lying face down on the floor behind the couch. When she turned him over, she gasped.

He was alive. Moving at least, and mouthing something she couldn't understand. Blood soaked his torn shirt and ran down the front of his chest. Something had ripped into him like a wild animal. And mixed within all the blood and torn cloth, there was something like dirt.

Not dirt. Ash.

The same stuff she'd found on herself after the attack in the parlor's parking lot.

The same person?

The gun sat several feet away, mixed in with everything else.

She didn't touch it.

The front door was closed, but before she did anything else, she stepped over to the door and locked it.

Then she broke down crying.

27

Ally arrived at her sister's house shortly after the ambulance had taken Daniel away. Nora had called her in a panic after the police had arrived, begging her to come over and watch Lucy for the night because they had to take Daniel to the hospital.

When Ally arrived twenty minutes later, there was still blood on the floor, with stains soaked into the carpet. Daniel's bloody shirt was lying in a heap near the door as if someone had discarded it on the way out.

Nora was ready to go as soon as Ally arrived, standing at the door with her keys in hand, a look of despair and fear on her face.

"Thank you for coming over." Nora glanced back toward the staircase. "Lucy's in her room. I'm not sure if she's sleeping."

"I'll take care of everything." Ally reached out and touched Nora's shoulder. "I don't mind at all. I'll check on her."

"Ally, I'm so—" Nora broke into tears. They embraced for a long moment until Nora pulled back and stepped toward the door. "Poor Lucy's been through so much lately, and you're the only one I could call on such short notice. The only one I trust."

"Don't be silly," Ally said. "This is a lot to handle, and you're my sister."

Nora nodded and wiped away a tear. "Daniel's pistol is in the kitchen. I put it in the drawer beside the refrigerator. I didn't know where else to put it after the police left. He usually keeps it locked up in our bedroom."

"I'm sure I won't need it."

"Still," Nora said, "keep it handy."

Ally watched her sister's face for a moment. Another tear ran down her cheek. "I'm sure whatever it was won't come back."

"Ally." Nora inched closer and met her sister's gaze. "Daniel refuses to say it, but I know something unnatural entered our house tonight. He said he shot them three times point blank, but they didn't go down." She fought to hold back more tears. "They nearly tore off his face. By the looks of it, they went for his eyes."

Ally stepped forward, and they embraced again.

After a few seconds, Nora finally pulled away. "If you have any problems—"

"I'll call the police right away," Ally finished, still holding her sister's arms.

A flash of pain swept over Nora's face. "Do you think I made a mistake?" she said. "By forcing you to destroy the statue? You said it might release something worse. Maybe you were right. This is worse."

The rising fear in Nora's eyes melted Ally's heart. She shook her head. "No. I'm sure it's not because of that."

Nora furrowed her brow. "Then what is it?"

"It's demonic." Ally tensed. "I'm sure of it."

"Something connected with Gabriel?"

Ally nodded again. "I think so."

"But we ended all that." Nora narrowed her eyes and inched closer. "You know what it is, don't you?"

Ally hesitated to answer. Would her sister believe the truth?

It was better to let it go for now. She shook her head. "I'm not sure of anything."

Nora's shoulders slumped. "What if it comes back?"

"It won't."

"How do you know?"

Ally stared into Nora's eyes and gave a reassuring smile. How could she tell her sister what she was planning to do? "I just do."

Nora nodded and then looked down. "If Lucy had gotten hurt—"

"She didn't." Ally flinched. She didn't want to think about what *might* have happened. "We'll get this figured out, I promise."

Nora seemed to calm a bit, taking in a shuddering breath. "I better get to the hospital. Daniel needs me. Lock the door after I leave. Use the deadbolt."

"I will." Ally scanned the area. The devastation was heartbreaking. It would take days to clean everything, but Lucy's trauma would take much longer to heal. "Did you see who—or what—it was?"

Nora hesitated to answer. "Not me. Only Daniel. But I heard him describe it to the police. Bigger and faster than he was. 'It was dark,' he told them a few times. Not much else. Earlier, I saw some shadows moving outside the window, but I didn't get a good look. Daniel isn't someone to act recklessly, especially not with a gun. He must have felt threatened. He never would have fired it unless he was certain."

Ally nodded and stroked her sister's arm. "You'd better get going. Don't worry about a thing."

Nora glanced back at the destruction. "I'm not worried about all this. *This* I can handle. I'm only worried about Lucy. The attack will traumatize her too, and I'm not sure how much more I can take."

"We'll get through this." Ally embraced her sister again.

"Are you sure?" Nora broke into more tears.

"Yes."

When Nora pulled away, she turned and wiped away a tear. Grabbing her car keys off the table beside the door, she trudged out the door but paused in the doorway. "Call the police if you see anything unusual. Don't wait."

"I won't let anything happen to her," Ally said. "I promise."

Nora nodded once, then shut the door and locked it behind her.

Turning back to face the broken house, she glanced toward the stairs. Lucy and Blanco were up there sound asleep and dreaming of rainbows and unicorns. The silence filled Ally's ears. She needed to take action before things got worse. She shuddered to think of what would have happened if she had listened to Nora and destroyed the statue. It would have left them with no options to defend themselves.

Lifting her purse from beside the door, she opened it. The statue was right there near the top. She lifted it out and stared at it for a moment. Its blackened eyes almost seemed to come to life.

"Let's finish this," she said.

❧ 28 ☙

Ally walked upstairs to check on Lucy, examining the trail of destruction along the way. The extent of the damage sent a chill down her spine. Something had made its way through the house, up the stairs, and all the way to Lucy's door. But then it had stopped.

The carpet was singed in several areas, but it was difficult to see without switching on more lights. Lucy's door was caved in, but the wood had held. Whatever had crashed into it had almost broken through and then stopped. Or something had stopped it?

If the intruder was unnatural, like Nora had suggested, then they weren't going to solve the problem by locking the door and grabbing a pistol. Whatever had gotten inside the house had entered with a clear purpose. They had known exactly where they were headed on their way up the stairs. They hadn't continued further down the hall toward Nora and Daniel's room. They had stopped right in front of Lucy's door.

And a thin layer of dust covered everything. Not dust—ash. It was subtle—she hadn't seen anything like it before—and almost invisible to the naked eye, except when viewed from the right angle. But it was there. Ash clung to every surface—the same type of ash she had seen in her vision.

She brushed her finger through some of it, and a smell floated into the air. Sulfur? Brushing away a little more, the signs of a faint symbol came through—the hollow flame. The one Gabriel had used for Moloch.

Her heartbeat quickened.

This was everything she had feared. She couldn't just ignore what she knew to be true—something was targeting Lucy, and Nora and Daniel were too blind to see the truth.

She had to do something—before things got worse.

Tess's words still echoed in her mind—everything about the statue, her purpose, and protecting Nora's family. Whatever had happened tonight only reinforced Ally's resolve to get this done, to follow through with her plans, to do it now. It was only going to get worse if she waited.

Nora wasn't going to solve this on her own.

It was up to Ally.

Peeking inside Lucy's room, Ally spotted the girl in her bed. Her little frame was outlined against the light of a small night-light near the floor. A pink comforter covered her, but it was pulled aside. She was awake, slowly stroking Blanco's fur. He was cuddled up near her chest but not purring.

Stepping over to Lucy, Ally crouched beside her niece and brushed the hair out of her face.

Lucy cracked her eyes open, but she didn't say anything. They stared at each other for a few seconds before the little girl's eyelids drooped again, and she started brushing Blanco's fur again. Her fingers moved slower and slower until finally stopping, and her breath settled into a steady rhythm.

It was hard to believe Lucy could have fallen back asleep so easily after another trauma like that. Hopefully, she hadn't encountered the attacker or seen the destruction.

I won't sit back and let it happen again.

Ally backed away from Lucy slowly and planned exactly what she needed to do. She would place the statue under Lucy's bed—the only way to ensure the girl was completely protected. But before she could do anything, she needed to get Blanco out of the room. Just having him nearby would needlessly complicate things. He would no doubt sense the statue's presence and have a severe reaction to it, like he had in Ally's apartment when his scar had erupted. If Lucy woke up to find him writhing in pain like that again, it would send the girl into a panic.

A cold weight settled into Ally's chest. She needed to focus. Was this really the best path forward?

The answer came back swiftly.

Yes.

Not just the best path—the *only* path.

The last thing Lucy needed was more trauma. She needed sleep—she deserved it.

Staring sympathetically at Blanco, he turned sharply toward her, staring back at her with his wide copper eyes, lit by the dim light coming in through the window. He sat motionless like that for several seconds.

Do you know what I'm thinking?

He didn't move.

I'm doing this for you too, you know.

His tail flicked once when she moved toward him. He pushed back against Lucy's chest as she reached out slowly to pull him away.

He let out a low growl.

"No," Ally whispered. "Not tonight. You can't be in here."

The cat withdrew further under Lucy's arm until Ally touched his fur. He stiffened, letting out another guttural growl, before lurching forward, swatting at her hands with a loud hiss.

Ally gasped and jumped back. What had gotten into him? Suddenly *she* was the bad guy?

I'm only trying to help.

Lucy stirred at the same time, and her breath paused.

Ally waited for her breath to return to a steady rhythm before trying to pull Blanco away again. This time, she reached in more slowly, watching his face while whispering, "It's okay, little guy. I'm just... We're both on the same side."

He allowed her to get close this time. With great care, she lifted Lucy's arm to separate them. At the same time, he jumped out of the bed. He landed a few feet away and paused beside the closet before turning back to face her. He stood there like that, silently still, with his gaze fixed on her.

Ally scowled in the darkness. It was bad enough that she'd almost awakened Lucy, but now Blanco wasn't cooperating.

How am I going to get you out of here?

It clearly wasn't going to be as easy as she'd expected, but at least the door was closed. He had nowhere to go.

She moved toward him again, this time grabbing him and holding him with both arms. He scratched at her forearms, even biting at her skin, although not deeply.

"Easy, little guy," she said, squeezing him against her chest. He didn't resist this time.

Before he had a chance to escape, she hurried him out of Lucy's room. Pulling the door shut with her elbow, she carried him down the hallway and dropped him inside the laundry room. He retreated to a spot beside his carrier and let out a soft meow.

"I'm sorry," she said. "It's just for one night. After this is over, we'll be friends again. I promise."

She backed away and closed the door between them.

As soon as the door clicked shut, her heart skipped a beat. There was nothing to stop her now. She could picture exactly what she was going to do—slide the statue underneath the bed, perform the brief ritual that Tess had provided, and step out of the room.

That was it.

Simple.

She'd brought the statue with her, stuffed it in her purse on the way out. She hadn't known why at the time, only sensing an intuitive tug to bring it along just in case. But it had seemed like the right thing to do. Now she was thankful that she'd listened to her instincts.

As soon as she'd heard her sister's panicked voice on the phone, she'd known something unnatural had happened, and it only made sense to bring it along. Just in case.

It was downstairs in her purse, and it would only take a few minutes to finish what she had started.

Heading downstairs again, she checked her phone first. No calls from Nora or Daniel. No doubt they would be at the hospital all night, judging by what Nora had said about his injuries.

She grabbed her purse and opened it. The statue was there at the bottom, buried beneath a pile of her personal items and wrapped in a towel.

She dug it out and scrutinized it like she'd never done before. It was amazing to think that this object held so much power. How did something like this work? It was just a carved stone, after all. But somehow it resonated with the darker vibrations—attuned to those things unseen.

Maybe she would never know how it worked, but it didn't matter. She'd seen its effect on Blanco and had felt its energy on a deep level. It worked.

Tess's words came back to her.

Just one night.

The instructions for the ritual came back to her with ease. The words streamed into her mind. This part wasn't so difficult —the phrasing was impossible to forget, given the research she'd already done on the box and statue. But the words needed to be vocalized in Lucy's room after the statue was in place. It was necessary, Tess had said, to get the statue as close to the child as possible, and there was only one place safe enough away from prying eyes—beneath Lucy's bed.

Carrying the statue up the stairs with great reverence, cradling it with both hands for most of the way, she opened Lucy's bedroom door and stepped inside. Her niece was still in the same position, with no signs that she'd noticed Blanco's absence. The girl's breathing was slow and steady, the precious sounds of an angel dreaming.

As it should be.

And your Aunt Ally will make sure that nothing unseen ever harms a hair on your head.

Just a couple of hours, while you sleep.

The statue's presence was enough. Powerful and effective. Like fighting fire with fire.

It was the only way.

Kneeling beside Lucy's bed, she placed the statue on the floor. Her hands trembled as she began the brief ritual in the silent darkness, opening the leather pouch that Tess had provided and dipping two fingers into it. The ash inside was cold against her skin, even colder when she lifted them out. Drawing a small circle on the floor with the tips of her fingers, she then placed the statue in the center and said the words:

"Sanguis custodia, verbum tenebris, nexum claude, ne transire."

Blood is the guard, word of shadow, seal the bond, let none pass.

Lucy's bedroom door was open, but it pushed open further, cracking against the doorjamb. The sound didn't awaken Lucy, thank God, but a surge of energy filled the room—unseen, cold, and heavy. A presence had entered. Someone was watching her from the shadows, its weight shifting against the floorboards. Every hair on the back of her neck stood on end.

Ezeran?

Moloch's emissary had arrived to protect Lucy.

She pressed her palms against the floor and leaned forward, reciting the words Tess had instructed slowly and carefully over and over in a whisper so soft, she could barely hear them herself.

Lucy shifted again in her bed. Ally paused until she settled and then continued when the girl didn't wake up.

Almost done...

A pulse of heat spread across the floor, surging through Ally's hands. The icy chill was gone, replaced by the faint smell of sulfur. Something was burning. She could see what looked like black smoke drifting through the air. It hadn't come from the kitchen—not from anywhere outside Lucy's room, but from the circle she'd drawn on the floor.

Lucy coughed twice and moaned in her bed.

Ally tried to wave it away. She hadn't started any fires or used anything flammable. She hadn't lit anything. Yet it continued rising until she spoke the last words from Tess's instructions:

"Clauditur porta. Vinculum manet."

The door is closed. The bond remains.

That was it. It was done.

She let out her breath and sat motionless, waiting, watching Lucy for any signs that she'd awakened from the disturbance. The girl had slept through everything.

After several minutes, the smoke cleared, although the dark presence remained. Ally avoided turning to face it, sensing that it was watching her. Her skin crawled. It hadn't left, but it hadn't moved to harm her either. Still, she could feel its gaze bearing down on her back.

They remained like that in a fragile stillness for a long moment, until she slid the statue beneath Lucy's bed, just as Tess had directed. All that was left was the long wait to retrieve it in the morning. It would sit under there like a sleepless sentry all night.

Nobody can harm you now.

Brushing away the ashes from the floor, Ally stood and stepped out of the room, closing the door behind her without looking back. After the door's latch clicked shut, she shuddered and let out a sigh of relief.

"I did it."

29

Nora helped Daniel get inside the house. After their long overnight stay at the hospital, they were both exhausted. The doctors had signed off on Daniel's discharge, but it wasn't the physical scars she was concerned about. He was still struggling to recover, with his arms and face a patchwork of bandages. Even now, he hadn't said much about what he'd seen.

On top of everything else, they'd waited endlessly to see a doctor in the emergency room, and then another hour to get the test results back. The ER doctor had said he was lucky—no broken bones, just bruises, cuts on his face, and a few stitches for the deeper cuts on his chest. "It could have been so much worse," they'd said. Daniel had only nodded at the diagnosis; the life drained out of his eyes.

At least they were home now, but the exhaustion showed on his face. Nothing had changed since they'd left. All the chaos was still there exactly as they'd remembered it, although Ally had cleaned up much of the glass and had straightened some of the furniture.

Daniel moved toward the kitchen with his head down, and Nora didn't stop him. He was probably starving. He hadn't eaten more than a few bites at the hospital.

Nora found Ally asleep on the couch in the living room. Her sister looked like the lone survivor of a wild house party. When Nora approached, Ally jumped to her feet.

"Sorry," Ally apologized. "I must have fallen asleep."

"It's okay." Nora laughed softly. "You can sleep all you want. Is Lucy upstairs?"

Ally rubbed her eyes, looked around, then nodded with a little grin. "She slept the whole time."

Nora stepped carefully over the broken coffee table and gave her sister a hug. "Thank you for staying with her."

"No worries." Ally beamed. "I'm just glad I could help."

"Lucy never came down?" Nora asked.

"No, but I checked on her every so often."

Nora glanced toward the stairway. The carpeting was soiled a lot worse than she remembered from the night before, but the damage was clear now. It looked as if someone had trudged up there wearing muddy shoes. "It's hard to believe this is real. It's like a war zone in here. Poor Lucy will see it every time she comes downstairs. She's already been through so much recently. She doesn't deserve this."

"Neither do you," Ally said, "but I think the worst is over."

Nora met Ally's gaze and lowered her voice. "What makes you think that?"

Ally hesitated and shrugged before answering. "It just feels... safe, don't you think?"

Nora stared at a shattered family portrait on the floor beside a fallen bookshelf. "No. Not at all."

"We're still standing," Ally continued. "Daniel must have scared them away. Whatever it was, it's gone."

"I wish I had your optimism right now."

"We did the best we could."

Nora moved closer to Ally. "I asked Daniel who he thought it was. He couldn't answer me."

"It was dark."

"That's what he said, but he shot them three times, Ally. Where's the blood?"

Ally stared across the floor and then shrugged. "You're still trying to rationalize this?"

"I have to, for my sanity. Does any of this make sense to *you*?"

"Our past is never far behind. I'm sure it's connected to something or someone we encountered—something supernatural—but we've turned the corner, right? The house was quiet all night, and I have a good feeling about our future." Ally glanced toward the kitchen. "I can help you clean up."

Nora shook her head. "We'll deal with everything later. It'll take a while to fix everything."

"Is Daniel all right?" Ally glanced back toward him. He looked up at the same time and then looked away.

"Neither of us slept at the hospital," Nora said. "The nurses kept coming in every ten minutes to check on him. My head was spinning by the time we checked out. I wasn't even sure I could drive home."

"I would have picked you up," Ally said.

"We got home."

Ally nodded and glanced toward the window. The morning light streamed in through the open blinds. She swallowed. "It's already morning."

Nora headed toward the stairs. "It feels like we've been awake for days. If you want to—"

A frenzied scratching noise came from the laundry room. Nora walked cautiously toward the door and cracked it open. Blanco jumped out and charged straight up the stairs.

"What the—? Why was Blanco in the laundry room?" Nora looked toward Ally for an explanation.

"He wouldn't calm down last night." Ally glanced away. "I didn't want him bothering Lucy, so I put him in there."

"He seems frantic."

"He was like that all night." Ally shrugged. "I suppose the attack affected him like everyone else."

Daniel returned from the kitchen after finishing his glass of water, groaning with every few steps. Nora went back to his side, checked the bandages on his face, and helped him toward the stairs with her arm under his.

Nora glanced back at Ally. "I'm sure you're exhausted too. You don't have to stay."

"I don't mind. Let me help."

Ally followed them up the stairs.

Nora stayed by Daniel's side and kept him steady. "You're almost there."

"I'm not sure how much I'll get done at the parlor today," he said.

"Forget the parlor," Nora said. "It can wait."

After they reached the top of the stairs, they all stopped in front of Lucy's bedroom door. The damage to her door sent a chill up her spine. It was shocking to see how close they had come to tragedy. Blanco was scratching at the door. He was pushing, meowing, and digging his paws along the bottom opening.

"He's worked up about something," Daniel said.

"He probably misses Lucy," Nora said.

Before Nora could open the door to let him into Lucy's room, Ally stepped forward and reached toward him, trying to pick him up. Blanco hissed at her instead, swiping at her hands.

"Blanco!" Nora called out. "Bad kitty!"

Blanco stood firm in front of the door, even as Ally tried to grab him again.

"He's been like this all night," Ally said with a little laugh. She struggled to move him out of the way. "You can see why I couldn't let him into Lucy's room."

Nora stared at the cat for a moment. "I haven't seen him this agitated in a while."

Daniel gave a little wave. "Leave him alone. Cats are like that —insecure." He turned to Ally with a solemn expression. "By the way, thank you for staying the night on such short notice.

I'm not sure what we would have done without you. I know I wasn't exactly pleasant yesterday. I regret a lot of the things I said."

Ally nodded sympathetically. "We both just want to keep Lucy safe."

"You can come over anytime," he continued. "It's just those drawings..."

"I don't blame you," Ally said. "I'm sure she won't be doing that anymore."

Daniel nodded with his head down.

Blanco started scratching at the door again, pushing at it over and over until the frame itself rattled.

"Blanco." Nora leaned down to pick him up. But he resisted her. He didn't hiss this time. Instead, he leaned into the doorway, pushing the full weight of his body against the door sideways.

Nora gave up and opened the door, letting him run inside. "I suppose it's okay if he goes in now. She's probably awake, anyway. Lucy?"

Lucy cracked her eyes open when they stepped inside, but the girl didn't sit up. "Mommy?"

Nora sat on the edge of Lucy's bed and pushed the hair out of the girl's eyes. "Did you sleep well?"

Lucy nodded. "I had a *wonderful* dream. I was running through a field of flowers."

Nora smiled. "I hope you have that dream every night."

Ally was smiling too.

Glancing around, Blanco had disappeared. Instead of jumping up on the bed with Lucy like he usually did, he'd gone somewhere out of sight. "Blanco?"

Ally kneeled beside Lucy's bed and reached under it.

"He's probably just playing a game," she said. "This is what I'm talking about. He's been like this all night."

Daniel came in a moment later and sniffed at the air. "What's that smell? Like a campfire in here." He looked at Ally. "You light a match or something? A candle?"

Ally shook her head and gave a dismissive wave of her hand. "It's been like that, after what happened."

Nora nodded. She'd also smelled it a moment earlier but had dismissed it as a residual of the intruder's presence. Now, it was impossible to ignore.

"Something's burning... in here." Daniel stepped forward, sniffing again, then dropped on his knees beside Ally and stared beneath the bed. "Blanco's got something under there. He's curled up beside something." He gestured for Blanco to come out, snapping his fingers. "Come here, little guy."

"I got him," Ally said, finally pulling Blanco out forcefully with both hands. He squirmed within her grasp until she pressed him tightly against her chest. But his eyes were wide, fixed on the darkness under Lucy's bed.

Daniel reached in further and pulled out a strange object. "What's this?"

Nora recognized it immediately.

The statue.

The one that had survived Father Tony's holy water baptism at the church. The demonic statue. The one Ally had destroyed in the parlor's parking lot. Here it was in perfect condition. Nora's heart skipped a beat. Her gaze jumped to Ally. "You... destroyed this."

"Nora, listen—"

"I watched you destroy this!" she cried out. "How did it get in here? Under Lucy's bed?"

Daniel stood again and scrutinized it. He looked confused until his face reddened, and he turned sharply toward Ally and glared at her. "You brought this in here, didn't you?"

She swallowed. "It's not what it seems. It's for her protection. After what happened last night—"

"Holy shit, I don't believe it!" Daniel shouted. "We trusted you with our daughter—with her life! And after what we talked about yesterday, you still went ahead and did *this*!" He squeezed the statue and raised it into the air.

Nora plucked it out of his hands before he had a chance to throw it through the window.

"I brought it here to keep her safe," Ally said. "You don't understand."

Daniel shook his head. "I don't believe it." He pointed toward the door. "Get out of here. I don't want to see you ever again. You're not welcome here anymore."

"No, Daddy!" Lucy cried out. "Don't say that to Aunt Ally!"

Daniel was trembling with rage.

Ally backed away, moving toward the door with her hands pushed together. "Please let me explain."

"Stop!" he shouted. "Just leave."

"I will." Her gaze jumped from him to Nora. "I'm sorry... but you don't understand—"

"We understand perfectly," he said. "We can't trust you. Now get out of here."

Nora's eyes welled up with tears and streamed down her cheeks. None of this made any sense. They *had* destroyed the statue, yet here it was in her hands. She struggled to grasp the flood of questions swirling through her mind. How? Why? She had watched Ally destroy it *right in front of her*.

Ally moved out into the hallway. Daniel followed her only a few steps behind.

Nora wiped away her tears and went out next, still clutching the statue in her hands. "Why would you do something like this?"

Ally glanced over her shoulder. "For all of you. At least Lucy's safe now."

Daniel nudged her forward. "We don't need your help. Never again."

He stopped at the top of the stairs, glaring down at Ally while she descended sideways with an apologetic expression.

Lucy tried to push her way past them, her face filled with fear and pain. She was crying too, but Daniel held her back.

"No, Mommy!" Lucy cried. "No, Daddy! Don't make Aunt Ally leave!"

Nora swept past Daniel and Lucy, following her sister down the stairs, if only to keep some distance between her and Daniel. Ally was crying now, too.

"I'm so sorry." Ally stepped down the stairs. "I had to. Someday, you'll understand."

"No, Mommy!" Lucy cried again.

"Go back to your room," Daniel said firmly to Lucy and then turned his focus back to Ally. "Lock the door after she leaves and never let her back in again."

Ally didn't look back when she reached the bottom. She headed straight for the door after grabbing her keys off a nearby nightstand beside the entrance. When she finally glanced back, her gaze dropped to the statue in Nora's arms. "I know I did the right thing."

Nora shook her head. "How could you do this to me?"

Blanco had followed them. He stopped beside Nora and stared up while letting out a loud hiss.

Nora rushed forward and thrust the statue into Ally's arms. "Daniel's right. We can't trust you anymore, and I never want to see that thing again. You betrayed me, Ally. How could you do that to us? You've ruined everything."

Ally shook her head and then opened the door to leave. "No. I just saved your lives."

❦   3 0   ❦

Ally sat alone in her apartment for the rest of the day. There was no point in leaving. The parlor was quiet all day, and nobody arrived to do any renovations. It wasn't just that Daniel had gotten injured in the attack the previous night and couldn't come in. They had abandoned her.

This was her punishment, she figured—a time out in her apartment to reflect on the awful thing she'd done, at least in their minds. They hadn't spoken since leaving her house that morning. No text messages, no calls, no communication at all.

They just didn't understand. Nora had treated her as if she were someone dangerous, as if she were a threat. And Daniel had practically shoved her out the door.

But she had done the right thing.

Hadn't she?

The statue seemed to agree. It sat in front of her now, facing her with those pitted eyes. There was just something about the statue's empty sockets that seemed to connect with her on a deeper level. The light bounced off the concave surface and refracted through the crystals along the rim, giving them an almost infinite depth. It was a trick of light, of course, yet at just the right angle it seemed to come to life.

A pile of Lucy's drawings sat nearby. All of them shared a similar theme—things her niece must have dreamed or seen—reflections of her imagination and fears. Just a girl expressing herself. Nothing unusual, at least for someone in *her* family.

At least... she wouldn't draw things like that anymore.

The real danger was gone.

She would get back to drawing rainbows and unicorns, just like Daniel wanted.

Nothing scary or unnatural.

She pulled out a chair at the kitchen table, leaned forward, and dropped her head into her hands.

You did the right thing, Ally. You protected them, even if they don't understand. One day, they'll thank you.

What did Nora think she would do in a situation like that? Just sit back and do nothing? Impossible. Who knows what would have happened to them—to Lucy—if Ally hadn't put the statue under Lucy's bed?

"I had to do it," she said to herself.

Still, Daniel's words echoed in her mind. She couldn't make them go away. His anger and the accusations of betrayal.

It had almost worked out perfectly—if only they hadn't come home too early.

She had almost made it through the night flawlessly.

She cringed. How had she so carelessly fallen asleep on the couch like that? Why hadn't she set the alarm on her phone as a backup for sunrise? Especially for something so important.

But how could she have known Nora and Daniel would come home that early in the morning? Didn't hospitals usually wait to discharge patients in the afternoon when the doctors made their rounds? But maybe emergency room procedures were different.

Her plan had been solid. But still... it had failed.

Silence did one thing—it gave her time to reflect on what she would do now.

Would her sister force her to move out of the apartment?

Would they ever let her talk to Lucy again?

How far would they take this?

The unanswered questions were heartbreaking. But she tried not to focus on the worst-case scenario. She would hope for the best, give them time to heal from what, in their minds, was a crime she had committed. And eventually, she would help them understand after the memory had faded.

She would help them see the reality of what she had done. The good that had come from her actions.

Holding the statue now was cold comfort. It had served its purpose. But what would she do with it? Would she ever need it again?

Regardless, she didn't want to keep it. It was better to give it back to Tess. Better to return it to where it had come from, where someone else could appreciate it. Tess would know what to do with it. And while she was there, Ally could thank the woman... for believing in her.

Ally was never meant to hang on to the thing forever, anyway. It was just passing through her hands on its journey to the next person who needed it. Just a tool, as Tess had described it.

The reality of what she had done would eventually come out —along with all the good that had resulted from her actions.

Ally looked at the time on her phone. Better to head out now before it got dark.

She stood and carried the statue across the kitchen before wrapping it in a kitchen towel. On her way to the back door, she grabbed her keys and then stepped out into the empty parking lot.

The sun had already gone down. She'd missed an entire day, not even going out for a coffee. A subtle wind blew across her face and through her hair. Even now, she sensed that something had changed. She no longer had the feeling that someone was watching her. Whatever had connected this place to the statue, it was now gone.

After climbing into her car, she sent Tess a quick text message, if only to give her a heads-up:

Sorry for the short notice. I'm going to stop by with the statue. It's better for you to keep it. I hope that's okay. See you soon.

She waited a moment for a reply. It didn't come.

No worries. It wouldn't take long to get to the woman's house, and seeing her in person again would be a perfect opportunity to say thank you for everything.

Within minutes, she was out on the road, heading toward Tess's house, with the statue lying on the passenger seat beside her.

When she pulled up in front of the woman's house, she shut off the engine and sat in silence for a few minutes. The neighborhood seemed more... empty than last time. It was a little darker too. The wind had died down, and one of the streetlights was out in front of Tess's house. The woman's home felt different this time. It was almost invisible behind the thick trees that filled her yard.

Walking up the sidewalk to the front door, the porch lights were on. A few lights were on in the house, and the front door... was open? Tess had somehow forgotten to close it.

Despite the open door, Ally paused and rang the doorbell. The sound echoed inside, coming from somewhere just around the corner.

Nothing.

"Hello?" Ally called into the house. "Tess?"

Nobody answered. She stood still and held her breath for a moment. Silence. Not even the sound of Eve's violin. The instrument was there. She could see it through the open door, just lying on the floor inside the house, along with the bow.

Had they left in a hurry?

Ally stepped forward and picked it up, taking only a few steps inside the woman's home before calling out a little louder, "Tess? Your door is open, so... I hope that's okay. This is Ally. Are you here?"

The hallway light was on, along with a room near the back.

Closing the front door, she walked over to the kitchen table and set down the violin. There were dishes all laid out—plates, glasses, silverware—all set for an evening meal. A pan of hot dish was simmering on the stove. The food inside was overcooked, so Ally switched it off.

Had they left in an emergency?

She took another glance around and then checked her phone again to see if Tess had replied yet to her text message.

Nothing.

"Tess?" she said again, even louder.

Still nothing.

Glancing around at the framed photos on the walls. She'd passed some of them on her previous visit. But the ones near the kitchen table she'd missed, along with a few drawings pinned to the wall beside them. Some of them were similar in theme to Lucy's dark drawings but clearly the work of a child. Eve must have created them.

One drawing stood out in particular—a familiar image, almost identical to one Lucy had drawn. It had the same shapes and colors—orange flames billowing from the windows of a tower, and shadowy figures standing in front of it.

Could they have had the same dream? How was that possible?

A chill swept down her spine.

Her phone rang, and she jumped. Digging her phone out of her purse, she stared at the screen.

Nora. She accepted the call, her heart racing.

"Hello?" Ally said.

"She's gone," Nora said in a frantic voice.

Ally took a moment to process what her sister had said. "What do you mean?"

"She's gone," Nora repeated. "Lucy is gone."

Nora awoke to the sound of Daniel snoring beside her in the bed. For a moment, she'd completely forgotten about the attack. But the faint smell of the hospital's bandages on his chest, arms, and face snapped her back to reality. It all came crashing back to her like a weight had settled onto her chest.

They had stayed home all day to give Daniel a chance to recover. By that afternoon, he'd calmed down enough to begrudgingly promise Lucy she could occasionally see Aunt Ally. They had shared a little family time that evening, just the three of them in the living room, straightening up from the attack, but Daniel could only sit back and watch them from his recliner.

At least the day had passed with no more trouble. They'd gone to bed early, but now she couldn't sleep. Turning onto her side, she glanced at her phone. It was almost midnight. She was exhausted, but her mind refused to switch off. On top of that, there was a strange energy in the air, and the back of her neck bristled.

She let Daniel sleep and climbed out of bed, then walked down the hall to Lucy's room. Her daughter's door was closed, and she opened it carefully.

Blanco darted out and ran past her, charging down the hall and then down the stairs without a pause.

Stepping quietly inside Lucy's bedroom, she found her daughter's bed empty. For a moment, it didn't seem real. There was a pile of crumpled sheets at the end of her bed that vaguely held the shape of her little frame. She walked over and pushed into them. But she wasn't there.

Nora stepped back out into the hallway and headed toward the bathroom. The light was off. Lucy would never go in there without turning on the light. Still, she walked over and peeked inside.

"Lucy?"

No answer.

There was a light on downstairs. Had Lucy snuck out of bed to grab a midnight snack? Or maybe she too couldn't sleep and had gone down to curl up in front of the television.

Heading down the stairs, there wasn't the usual sound of the television blaring cartoons. It was off, along with all the lights, except for the one light near the front door.

"Lucy?" she said again.

No answer.

She held her breath and listened for any signs of life.

Only the sound of her beating heart. Where could Lucy have gone? She switched on every light on her way to the kitchen. Was Lucy hiding in a corner or playing a game with Blanco?

But Blanco was standing like a guard at the door.

"Lucy!" Nora said with more authority. "Where are you? Come out here right now!"

Still nothing.

She hurried to the front door, and Blanco perked up when she turned the knob. It was unlocked. She pushed Blanco out of the way, cracked it open, and stuck her face through the opening. Lucy wasn't on the porch or in the front yard.

Panic erupted in her mind.

Oh my God, where is she?

Blanco scratched at the door and nudged up against her leg.

"No, Blanco." Nora shut the door before he could escape, then charged back up the stairs and switched on every light in every room until finally returning to her bedroom. Despite the commotion, Daniel was still asleep. She hated to wake him, especially after all that had happened.

"Daniel," she said in a gasp. "I can't find Lucy."

He grumbled and turned to face her. "Lucy? Isn't she in her room?"

"No." Nora tried to stay calm. "I can't find her anywhere."

"Just look for Blanco," he said.

She shook her head. "Blanco's downstairs. Alone. The front door was unlocked."

"Unlocked?" His eyes shot open, and he sat up. He winced, touching his chest where the doctor had stitched and bandaged his wounds. Struggling to climb out of bed, he didn't complain. When he finally stood, his face was full of fear and confusion. "Why is it unlocked?"

She didn't answer.

Stepping out into the hallway, they split up. He hurried through Lucy's bedroom and the bathroom, just as Nora had done, then rushed down the stairs.

"Lucy! Where are you?" he called out. "Get out here right now!"

Nora caught up with him down in the living room. He was opening every closet door, while Nora hurried down to their cramped basement. No sign of her down there either. When she came back up to the main floor, Daniel was standing outside on the porch. Blanco was watching him through the screen door. He was scraping his paws against it frantically. Nora stepped outside and stood beside him.

Daniel turned to face her. "Did she go outside?"

Nora shook her head. "I didn't hear anything. She might have been sleepwalking."

"Oh God, I hope not." Fear flashed across his face.

He charged down the steps and around the side of the house. "Lucy! Lucy!"

She followed him and scanned every tree and bush at the edge of their property.

After making a full circle around the house, they returned to the front steps.

Nora's heart was pounding. "We should call the police."

He nodded. "But... call your sister first. See if she walked to the parlor. Maybe she went there."

Nora nodded. Dialing her sister's number, she turned toward the neighbor's lawn. If Lucy wasn't in the house, then she must have wandered outside. How far could she have gone? If Lucy had gotten dressed and walked outside right after they'd gone to sleep, she could have made it across town by now.

Ally answered on the third ring.

"Hello?" Ally said in a cautious tone.

"She's gone," Nora said in as calm a voice as possible.

"What do you mean?"

"She's gone," Nora repeated. "Lucy is gone. I don't know where she went. We fell asleep after you left. We were so exhausted. And when we woke up... Ally, I can't find her. We think she left the house. Do you know where she might have gone? Is she there with you? Please tell me she's with you. Please."

"She's not with me." Ally gasped. "But I'm not at home right now. Are you sure she's not hiding somewhere? She likes to cuddle with Blanco in her closet."

"She's not with Blanco." Nora's voice wavered. "We already looked in her room, in her closet, in the basement. She's not in the house. She's not... anywhere."

Ally went silent for a moment. "I'll be there in five minutes... to help... if you want."

Nora glanced at Daniel. The panic was clear on his face, and even suggesting that Ally might come over in that moment would send him over the edge. She shook her head, even though her sister couldn't see her. "That's not a good idea. Even now. Please, just call me if you see her. We think she might have wandered outside to find you."

"I will," Ally said.

Daniel stepped forward, gesturing to the phone with tears in his eyes. "Let me talk to her."

Nora hesitated to hand him the phone, but desperation had replaced the anger on his face, and his hands trembled while holding it up to his ear. "Ally, please tell me that Lucy's with you."

The expression of hope on his face collapsed. A moment later, he spoke in a softer tone. "So if you're not at the parlor, where are you?" Another brief pause, then his shoulders slumped. "Call us if you see her." Ending the call, he handed the phone back to Nora.

She didn't say a word until they'd gotten back into the house. Blanco tried to push his way outside again when they walked in, but they held him back.

Nora gestured to him. "He's desperate to get outside. She must have gone out there... alone."

"Your sister has something to do with this. I know it."

Nora shook her head. "Don't say that. She would never do anything to hurt Lucy or take her without permission or anything like that."

"I don't know," Daniel said. "How can you be sure?"

"Because I *know* her."

"I can't trust her anymore," he said. "Maybe she told Lucy to meet her somewhere or talked her into—"

"Stop," Nora said sharply. "You know that's not true."

"After sneaking that thing under Lucy's bed—"

"Stop."

But on some level, Nora wasn't so sure. A shadow of a doubt had crept in. She couldn't be completely sure of anything anymore. How far would Ally take things? It was impossible to know. Things had spiraled out of control.

Daniel hurried upstairs and came back down a minute later

wearing the same clothes he'd worn after coming home from the hospital. Despite the exhaustion on his face, he grabbed his keys near the door and handed Nora hers. "Drive around the neighborhood, but stay close to the house. I'm going to the parlor. If she's not there, then maybe she's still on her way."

"We should call the police now."

He nodded. "I'll call them from my car. Call me as soon as you find her. Don't lock the door in case she comes back. Maybe even leave a note on the door for her to call us."

Daniel left.

Nora dressed quickly, and on her way out she fought to keep Blanco from escaping. If she let him outside, would he lead her to Lucy? Or would he run off, never to be seen again? She couldn't take the chance.

"You need to stay here, Blanco," she said. "Lucy would never forgive me if I lost you. I'm sure we'll be right back... with Lucy."

$$\text{❧} \quad 3\,2 \quad \text{❧}$$

Immediately after ending her phone call with her sister, Ally stared at the glowing screen until it went dark. Panic swept through her chest, along with shame, regret, and helplessness, knowing that Lucy had gone missing, and that she might have had something to do with it. She desperately wanted to run to Nora's house and do everything in her power to help find her niece. But her sister's words still echoed in her mind: "Don't come here. Not yet."

She had pissed off Daniel, and it would take some time for him to get past what he considered an unforgivable sin—placing the statue in Lucy's bedroom.

Ally turned toward the door with the phone still in her hand.

She couldn't just sit back and do nothing. She would go to the parlor first, to see if Lucy had somehow walked there on her own, then drive up and down every street all night if she had to. Daniel couldn't stop her from helping.

Still, the nagging voice at the back of her mind continued.

This is your fault.

But everything Ally had done was only meant to help the girl come to terms with the reality of where she'd come from and who she was. It was her *destiny*.

It's your fault.

Ally put away her phone and took a few more steps toward the exit. She stopped. Some items on an antique hutch near the dining room caught her eye—a line of carved figures Tess had laid out like little trophies. Ally hadn't noticed them before. Or maybe they hadn't been there before.

She stepped toward them to get a better look. There were several small figurines made of stone, metal, and what looked like ivory. Behind them sat a sepia-toned picture of a river, its banks lined with trees surrounding what looked like the ruins of an old rock quarry. There were no people in the photo, but judging by some cracks in the paper and the faded image, someone must have taken the photo at least a hundred years earlier.

Another photo sitting nearby showed the same location from a different angle. This one centered on a large stone tower in the foreground. It had the air of a castle tower in medieval times, and at its base sat a circle of smaller stones surrounding what looked like a fire pit with a large boulder in the center with a flat top. Someone had painted a crucifix and other demonic symbols across the stones.

It looked like someone had clipped it out of an old magazine or off the internet because of the grainy, crooked text printed just beneath it—just a few words—describing it as an incinerator in an abandoned rock quarry. Beside it sat another yellowed newspaper clipping. The headline, "Unholy Discovery at Hollow Bend Quarry," caught her attention. It was followed by a brief description of what the police had found there and ended with warnings for would-be trespassers to stay away.

The tower stood like a chimney, with two blackened windows near the top. The connection to Lucy's drawings was undeniable. This was the tower she had drawn—the "black-eyed house," as she'd called it. Not a house at all, but an incinerator—sitting abandoned in the middle of a forest.

Why had her little mind drawn *that*?

And how had she even known about its existence? She couldn't have imagined those details without having seen it on TV or the internet. But in Lucy's drawings, the tower was alive with fire—with darkened figures peering out at her through the windows.

Of all the things Lucy had drawn, that image had disturbed Ally the most. Now, it sent a chill up her spine.

Tess had collected these photos and figures, prominently displaying them along with everything else as if she were proud of them. Cherished items connected to her past?

Picking up one of the small stone statues on the hutch, Ally ran her fingers over the surface. Limestone? It had the same smooth texture, the same feel and color—although this one showed no signs of burn marks—and a similar weight as the statue she'd placed under Lucy's bed.

Another figure was seated on something like a throne with its eyes gouged out, blackened holes that seemed to hold endless depth. It was the same horrific imagery that Lucy had drawn on the wall in the parlor, as if she had somehow used the objects as reference. A perfect depiction.

All the stone items were aesthetically the same, so where had Tess acquired them? But it wasn't just the stone objects. The other items on the hutch were similar to what Ally had received from Father Tony. There were charms, smaller statues, and even another wooden box resembling the one Father Tony had burned with holy water at the church.

Something was wrong.

All wrong.

These were too clean. Too modern. Someone had created these by hand. They were scratched and weathered, but they weren't worn away by time.

Not ancient relics—these were created by someone recently. Her mind flashed back to what Tess had said about someone having crafted it from stone long ago. But maybe not *that* long ago. Had Tess sculpted them from limestone extracted from the quarry she'd mentioned earlier?

Ally stared at them until she caught sight of a framed color photo on the wall. It showed the quarry again. This photo was a little larger, except Tess was in it.

In this photo, she was much younger—a young woman in her twenties—standing alone in front of the tower, holding out what looked like a large oblong stone in her hands. She was extending it reverently toward the camera. Whoever had snapped the photo had captured Tess in what appeared to be one of the proudest moments of her life, judging by the expression on her face.

The stone in Tess's hands was roughly the same size as the one Ally had placed under Lucy's bed. It had the same form, and even without proof, it was clear that this was the same stone Tess had used to create the limestone statue.

The woman hadn't acquired it from some mysterious source. Not passed down through the centuries. Not some ancient relic.

Tess had made it.

Tess had created everything.

All of it—just a hoax? Or something darker?

But *why*?

Tess had given the statue to Gabriel to carry out his intentions. And now she'd passed it along to Ally. But was it even real?

It *had* to be real. She had seen what'd happened to the box in the church with Father Tony—how the holy water boiled over and burned the priest's clothes. It worked, at least, on *some* level. So why had Tess lied about its origins? For what purpose?

Ally turned back toward the hallway, focusing on the light coming from the open door near the back.

"Tess?" she called out one more time, and then headed toward it without waiting for a response.

Stepping into a small office lined with books, relics, and photographs, she stopped in front of a heavy oak desk in the center. Its surface was crammed with more relics, open books, loose papers, and old photographs. Among the clutter, she spotted a familiar name.

Gabriel.

His name was scrawled across the cover of one notebook, and Ally didn't hesitate to open it. Inside she flipped through pages of notes that detailed the man's life and his family. Everything was there, including detailed instructions for how he was to invoke the demon Moloch. Near the bottom of one page, after some notes about each of his dogs, she'd scribbled a single word.

Failure.

The handwriting was the same jagged script she'd seen on the note she'd found inside Gabriel's box.

And then more notes below that.

Moloch rejected the animals. It will require human sacrifice.

A flurry of sketches filled the margins of each page, and more detailed drawings of the Gabriel's box, each new version more intricate than the last. Turning another page, a photograph slipped out. It showed a younger Gabriel standing beside his daughter, his girl's hand resting on a dog's head—the German shepherd. Someone had blotted out its eyes in thick red ink.

A chill ran up Ally's spine. Tess hadn't helped Gabriel—she had used him. The ritual hadn't failed because of anything he'd said or done. It had failed because she'd used him as a trial run for her own twisted ambitions. Had she sent him to perform the ritual alone, knowing failure meant death if Moloch wasn't appeased?

Ally struggled to grasp the twisted reality of everything she was staring at. She pulled out her phone again and dialed her sister's number.

It rang and rang and rang—

Nora answered a moment before the voicemail picked up. "Hello?"

"Nora?" Ally said. "You have to meet me somewhere. I think I know where Lucy went."

"Where is she?" Nora asked in a desperate voice.

"I can't explain everything right now, but I need you to go there right now."

"Yes, of course." Nora paused for a moment. "How do you know this?"

"I just know. In the pictures Lucy drew... it's the incinerator near an old quarry in Minneapolis. Tess has her, Nora."

"Who's Tess?"

"Someone who I let whisper in my ear far too long. I'll text you the address now, but you need to get there as soon as you can. And bring the police with you."

"I will," Nora said. "Ally— Is she okay?"

Ally didn't answer. "Get there as fast as you can."

❦ 33 ❦

Nora waited for Daniel to finish speaking to the officer before breaking into their conversation. "Daniel, can I talk with you for a minute?"

They were all standing on the front lawn. Daniel was trying to explain everything to the officers in a way that wouldn't make him appear irresponsible, but he was getting too emotional. His words weren't coming out quite right.

"I'll be right back." They stepped away from everyone and met her gaze. "What do you need?"

"I talked with Ally," she said.

At the sound of her sister's name, Daniel flinched, but he didn't look away.

Nora continued, "She thinks she knows where to find Lucy."

He shook his head slowly. There was doubt in his eyes, and she didn't blame him.

The police had scoured the neighborhood and talked with most of the neighbors by then. They'd contacted anyone even remotely connected to Lucy. Nobody had seen the girl, and despite the repeated reassurances coming from the officers, her hope was fading.

"Where?" he asked skeptically.

"I have the address." She gestured toward her phone. "It's not far from here."

His expression softened a bit. "How does she know? Is she there with Lucy?"

"No."

His shoulders wilted, and the skepticism returned. "Then how does she know?"

Nora shook her head. "I'm just passing along what she told me. She wants us to meet her there and bring the police with us."

Daniel glanced back at the officer standing near them and turned away from him before continuing, "You didn't answer my question. How does she know?"

"I don't know."

He moved her away from the others and lowered his voice. "I'm not sure how they would react if I told them my psychic sister-in-law has a *hunch* Lucy is somewhere nearby. What's the address?"

"It's down near the river. An old quarry."

Daniel furrowed his brow. "Why would Lucy go to a quarry?"

"Ally didn't have time to explain," she said. "She told us to meet her there... with the police."

Daniel stepped in a little closer, his expression full of suspicion. "If Ally has any leads—*real* leads—I'll tell them about it. But if it's just a hunch..."

"Shouldn't we at least check it out? We should tell the police."

"All right." He nodded. "Yes, of course, but they're going to ask how Ally knows."

Nora shrugged. "We'll leave that to her."

They returned to the assigned officer and relayed the little information Ally had provided. The officer seemed to take everything seriously, writing down the address and Ally's contact info, but paused when Nora couldn't say more.

"We'll have one of the officers check it out," the officer said.

"My sister told us to go there right away," Nora said.

"I understand." He nodded. "We'll take care of it. It's better for you to stay home and let us check it out. They'll dispatch an officer right away."

"Should we... meet you there?" Nora asked.

The officer shook his head. "Every officer in the area is searching for your girl, and an Amber Alert went out a moment ago. We'll follow up with every lead, I promise."

Daniel didn't seem to hear what the officer had said and continued, "Who took her to a quarry? And how does Ally know all of this?"

The office stayed silent, but he was paying close attention to Nora's expression.

"I don't know, Daniel," she said. "I'm just trying to find our daughter. That's all Ally said, but we should at least go there and see what she's talking about."

"It's better for you to remain at home," the officer repeated, "in case we have questions."

Nora stared out over the dark streets. It was horrifying to think that her daughter was out there somewhere, alone and in danger. How could she be expected to just sit at home waiting for news of her return? This wasn't something she could leave to the police or anyone. She had to get out there herself and look for her daughter. Nothing they could say would hold her back.

Without saying another word, she headed back into the house. A few officers near the door glanced at her, but she didn't stop. She grabbed her purse and car keys from the table just inside the door and then hurried back outside with her gaze fixed on her car in the driveway.

"Babe?" Daniel asked as she passed him. "Where are you going?"

She glanced over her shoulder. "I texted you the address."

She didn't wait for him. Within minutes, she was out on the road. She couldn't help but drive too fast while scouring the sidewalks and yards along the way to the quarry. After she got out onto the main road, she couldn't stop thinking of Lucy. Her daughter might be hurt right now. Maybe lost and crying. Maybe held hostage by some sick person with nefarious intentions.

Or maybe it was all connected to that thing they'd found under Lucy's bed?

The mental images sent flashes of panic through her body, but she pushed them away. She had to.

She just got lost. Ally's wrong—nobody took her. Certainly not a stranger. That rarely happened anyway. There was a simple explanation. Lucy had gone to find Blanco after we all went to bed, and she went outside looking for him, thinking he'd gotten lost. She couldn't have gotten far—certainly not the eight miles to the old quarry. She's okay. I know it. She's okay.

Endless chatter flooded her mind.

Using GPS, she finally turned down the narrow road leading to the park beside the river. There was a sign near the front gate that read, "Park Closed After Dark—Violators Will Be Prosecuted," although the gate was wide open and left swaying in the breeze as if the city hadn't locked it in years. There was no sign that anything like a quarry lay ahead, but the GPS did show a river nearby.

At the end of the road, she stopped beside the only other car, and it belonged to Ally. Her sister was standing alone beside her car, her arms folded beneath a single light beaming down on her. The park, and everything else around her, was dark.

There was no sign of anyone else along that stretch of the river, including Lucy. Nora's heart sank. Had she made another colossal mistake by trusting Ally again?

She climbed out of the car and headed toward her sister with cautious optimism.

"Where is she?" Nora asked, folding her arms over her chest.

"We have to hurry." Ally gestured toward the river. "I haven't seen her yet, but I know she's down there."

Nora glanced down at the object in Ally's arms. Despite the dim light, she could make out its outline. The statue. "Is that what I think it is?"

"Yes," Ally said without explanation. "Just trust me. Lucy is down there."

"How do you know?" Nora forced herself to keep her voice down.

Ally took a step toward her. "Tess must have parked further down the road somewhere. Or maybe she knows a different path to get down to the quarry—I don't know. Are the police coming?"

"They said they would," Nora replied.

"Where's Daniel?"

"He's with them," is all she said.

Ally nodded and gestured toward the tree line then hurried toward it. "We have to get down there. There's an incinerator. Something's on fire. I can smell the smoke, and you can see the flames through the trees."

Nora strained to see anything within the darkness below them, but she *could* smell smoke. "Are you sure it's not just some campers or a homeless encampment?"

Ally shook her head. "No, you don't understand. This is the place Lucy was referencing in her drawings on the walls and in her art. Tess was obsessed with this place too. Somehow, every-thing connects back to here. This is where it all started—where Tess got the statue."

"She found it here?"

"Either that, or... she made it."

"How do you know all this?"

"I was inside her house when you called. But we don't have time, just... trust me, okay? You have to go down there with me right now, Nora. We can't wait for the police to arrive. I was hoping they'd be here by now, but I'm worried if we don't get down there soon something terrible is going to happen."

Nora stared into her sister's eyes and then nodded once. "All right. I'll follow you, but did you at least bring a weapon?"

"A weapon?" Ally shook her head. "I didn't go home. I came straight here."

"*If* someone took Lucy down there, they might be armed," Nora whispered.

"I know," Ally replied, glancing back at the road. "Goddammit, where are the police? But I don't think Tess anticipated anyone following her. We only need to disrupt what she's planning to do, and get Lucy out of there."

Nora glanced down at her purse. Without hesitating, she dug inside and pulled out the Smith & Wesson 9mm handgun Ally had placed in there after the first attack in the parking lot. She'd gotten used to the extra weight over the last few days and had forgotten it was even there.

"Brilliant!" Ally said.

"The one you gave me."

Ally looked at her cautiously. "Are you okay to use it?"

"I will," she said, holding it down and away from them, "if I have to." She turned back toward the fire. "This Tess woman... What do you think she's planning to do?"

"I'd rather not say," Ally said, turning away. "Just... keep the gun handy. Let's go."

Ally charged ahead, and Nora followed her down the trail. The branches scraped against their clothes and across Nora's bare arms. Mosquitoes buzzed incessantly around them. She hadn't prepared for this. They could use their phones in flashlight mode, but that would ruin the element of surprise. At least the moonlight overhead provided a little clarity. But that wouldn't help them if they encountered any wild animals or something worse. They wouldn't see the danger until it was almost too late.

They stayed silent, careful to avoid stepping on any branches that might give away their presence. A moment later, the fire-light Ally had mentioned finally came into view between the trees ahead. It was a soft orange glow, like someone's campfire. Ally was right.

She couldn't see anyone, but she heard a voice. A woman was speaking in a low, steady tone over and over, like a Gregorian chant in a foreign language.

They slowed near the end of the trail when the river came into view. The sound of its rushing water grew louder as they emerged into a clearing. Piles of rubble sat along the banks of the river, with the remnants of the old quarry straight ahead. A line of rusted construction equipment and a large wooden shed stood on one side of a wide, open pit. It was half-swallowed by weeds and graffiti. The place had sat abandoned for a long time.

Another menacing structure stood on the other side—the incinerator, lit at its base with the fire they'd seen through the trees burning. Two windows near the top glowed with embers from the flames.

Another road wound around the back of the pit, and at the end of it sat another car. Tess's?

Three people stood in front of the fire.

A woman who could only be Tess, her daughter Eve in a wheelchair, and Lucy.

34

Ally gasped at the horrifying scene in front of them. Nora started to lunge forward, but Ally threw her arm out and held her sister back.

"Wait," she whispered. "Not yet."

The sight of Tess holding Lucy hostage cut straight through Ally's heart. She had trusted the woman. Their conversations flooded back. Ally had followed every bit of guidance the woman had given her without hesitation. But the truth was clear now. It was all just a setup, and she had taken the bait every step of the way. She had blindly opened this dark door. She had facilitated this woman's true intention.

The reality stabbed at her heart. The pain welled up inside her chest, but she pushed it all back down. She had no other choice. Lucy still needed her.

An uncomfortable energy hung in the air. Something dark and tangible. Ally recognized it from their previous encounter at Gabriel's house.

Ally considered their options. They could sprint out into the open to rescue Lucy, but there was no telling what Tess might do. The woman was clutching a knife in her hand—the same one with the ivory handle she'd seen on Tess's dining table during their first visit. It was better to pause for a moment, if only to catch their breath and plan their actions. The stakes were too high.

Lucy was there, lying vulnerable on a stone slab. She was dressed only in her pink pajamas in front of the incinerator with her arms hanging limp at her sides. Her chest was rising and falling in a steady rhythm. At least she was alive. Her small face stared up at the night sky.

Tess stood beside her facing the incinerator. She was carefully maneuvering around a patchwork of candles arranged within a larger circle of stones that surrounded them. The formation mirrored the sigil Gabriel had burned into Blanco's flesh. Even from that angle, Ally could see it also matched the one carved into the lid of the box that had once held the statue. The candles burned brightly around them, yet the breeze sweeping in off the river didn't blow them out. Nothing about that place was natural.

Eve was sitting ten feet away. She was slumped forward in her wheelchair with her mouth hanging open and her limbs twitching in broken spasms. Her face was gaunt. If she were aware of her surroundings, then she wasn't struggling to escape.

Tess hovered between them like a conductor, making wide gestures with her arms. She seemed to draw energy from the incinerator's fiery glow and from the circle of stones around them. The woman cried out a series of Latin phrases. Each syllable filled the air with a guttural cry that could only come from a desperate, heartsick mother.

Ally recognized some of the words. She'd translated bits and pieces of the text earlier from the parchment, and it chilled her to think Tess was reciting them in the same way Gabriel must have done before sacrificing his dogs to Moloch.

It was clear Tess intended to do the same.

Ally tensed when Tess lifted the knife toward the darkened sky and shouted another string of Latin. Nora raised her gun at the same time. But instead of plunging the knife into Lucy, Tess stepped over and kneeled in front of Eve, whispering something in the girl's ear.

They embraced for a moment, even as Eve remained unmoving.

Her mother then wheeled Eve forward, pushing the chair up beside the stone slab with Lucy. Tess leaned her daughter sideways until her frail body slumped against Lucy. Lifting Eve's limp hand, she placed it at the center of Lucy's chest, then pressed it gently over the girl's heart. Lucy remained motionless throughout it all.

Tess whispered a few soft words—an incantation—over the two girls, the words swept away in the wind rising off the nearby river.

"If she tries to hurt Lucy—" Ally whispered.

"I'll shoot her dead before she has a chance," Nora said.

Tess picked up a small silver bowl, placed it beneath Eve's arm, then pulled her daughter's wrist forward. Using the knife in a swift, dispassionate motion, she sliced a clean line across the girl's inner wrist. Eve twitched, but she didn't scream. Instead, she let out a soft sigh as the blood spilled down her arm in a smooth red ribbon and pooled in the bowl.

Her mother grabbed a cloth from the back of the wheelchair and tied it around her daughter's upper arm like a tourniquet. Within seconds, the blood slowed, and she added a bit of gauze to seal her daughter's skin again. She did everything in a graceful, tender way. Then she dipped another larger white cloth into the bowl.

Lucy convulsed. Her body rose and fell against the stone, with her back arching as she clenched her teeth.

Eve seized and her small hand spasmed against Lucy's chest. Eve's chair rattled violently on its wheels and nearly tipped over. Tess dropped the knife, and the metal blade clinked against the stone ground. She wrapped her arms around Eve's chest and neck, and struggled to keep her daughter seated.

"Yes," Tess said. "You feel it now, don't you? It won't be long now. He's almost here, coming to make you whole."

Ally glanced back toward the top of the hill. There was still no sign of the police. But Tess was unarmed—it might be their only chance. Nora was already pushing forward again. With Tess's attention still on Eve, Ally turned to Nora. "We won't let her touch Lucy again."

"No," Nora said, "we won't."

They broke from the trees in unison, sprinting through the grass onto the quarry's ground. Their shoes crunched over the gravel and dirt while Ally's heart pounded in her chest.

Tess didn't flinch at Eve's side. She didn't even look up.

Nora reached the altar first, tearing the ropes off Lucy's wrists with one hand, while aiming the pistol at Tess with the other.

Ally arrived a moment later, but she stumbled along the way. The statue slipped from her hands and hit the ground with a loud crack. It came to rest facing up just a few feet outside the circle, but she didn't bother to retrieve it. It wasn't important anymore. Instead, she hurried to Lucy's side and tried to wake the girl. She wasn't responding, but at least her body was warm.

"Lucy," Ally said, "let's get you out of here."

"She's not waking up!" Nora cried out, smearing away the blood from Lucy's stomach with the edge of the girl's torn pajamas.

Ally glanced back at Tess. The woman still hadn't reached down to grab her knife. What was she waiting for?

At least there was still time to get Lucy out of there.

Nora scooped the girl into her arms, keeping the pistol pointed toward Tess at all times, and turned toward the trees. It wouldn't be easy to carry the girl up the hill, but they were younger and faster than Tess, and she doubted the woman would leave her wheelchair-bound daughter behind to chase after them.

Only... Tess still hadn't reacted *at all* to their presence. Did she know something they didn't? Ally glanced at the stones and candles surrounding them. The truth hit her like a punch to the gut.

"Wait." Ally grabbed her sister's arm. "We're trapped."

Nora's face twisted. "No," she said sternly, "we're not."

"We are." Ally gestured to the stone circle.

Nora followed her gaze. "Are you kidding me?"

Ally shook her head. "Lucy will never wake up again if you take her out of the circle. Whatever this is. Tess knows we can't leave. None of us can. Not until it's complete."

Tess nodded slowly, and a grin spread across her face. The woman had heard everything but had never left her daughter's side. Eve was still convulsing, with her mother doing her best to comfort her.

"Let it go, dear," Tess said to Eve. "It's all part of the process. You have nothing to fear and everything to gain. Just let it all in."

Nora inched toward the edge of the circle while clutching Lucy tighter in her arms. Was she planning to break the circle?

Before she could take another step, Ally touched her arm. "Trust me. This ritual... It's the same one Gabriel did before he sacrificed his dogs. I'm sure of it. Tess instructed him what to do, every detail, but he botched the steps somehow. Things won't go well if we leave now."

"When?" Nora asked sharply. "When can we leave?"

Nora was staring at her—waiting for an answer, for hope—but Ally didn't have the parchment anymore. It had gone up in flames, along with the box, but... she *had* taken a picture of it on her phone, hadn't she?

She dug out her phone and flicked through the photos until she found it—the parchment written in a mix of Latin and Hebrew text. She'd only had time to translate some of it, but there wasn't enough time now to complete it.

Skipping past what she knew to be the binding part of the ritual now, she paused near the bottom, focusing on a line scrawled in blood-ink near the bottom edge, almost obscured by burn marks. She translated the text on-the-fly.

"Iseth el'barim. Ana'el tal shur molochai."

Roughly translated, she understood it meant to break the chain of the demon Ezeran and return to dust. She recited the words, speaking them slowly and enunciating every syllable with care—but then stopped.

Tess wasn't trying to stop her. The woman was still fixated on her daughter. She wasn't doing anything to prevent Ally from aborting the ritual. Something wasn't right.

Maybe she hadn't said the words right, or she'd misunderstood their meaning. Repeating them over in her mind.

Still, the truth became clear.

Everything Tess had instructed her to recite in the apartment and beside Lucy's bed, they were only intended to call on the demon Ezeran.

It wasn't for anyone's protection, as Tess had convinced her. Everything was a lie.

Her hands went cold. "No. This isn't right."

"What's not right?" Nora asked.

She turned to face Tess. "I wasn't protecting Lucy at all. I was calling on the demon instead, wasn't I? You had me mark Lucy in the apartment after our first visit, then you had me bind her to him in her bedroom. *I* invited him in. *This* is how you tricked me."

"*Now* you understand?" Tess said sharply. "You must have spoken the words perfectly, because it's all moving along quite well. Thank you, Ally. I couldn't have done it without you."

Ally's mouth dropped open. "But the words I read just now from the parchment... I broke the tether."

"Much too late. Gabriel almost did it right, but when he failed, I had to move on to the next one. I can't do this myself, you know. It requires someone with a pure intention—intention is everything, you know—but mine... My soul is far too corrupt for this sort of thing. You provided Ezeran with a door and then guided him right through it. You even marked the girl for me. I just needed one vessel, and you provided the perfect opportunity—you, your sister, and... little Lucy. And when you came knocking on my door to ask for help... oh, it was too much to resist. You summoned him to the child's soul."

Ally's stomach dropped as the dark truth sank in. "I'm so sorry," she said again to Nora.

"Of course, you are, dear. And now..." Tess stared into the fire raging at the base of the incinerator. "He is here."

35

Ally stared at the incinerator's mouth. The flames burst higher when Tess began reciting a string of words, erupting as if someone had tossed gasoline onto them. The woman spoke with her eyes closed. Had she memorized the lines? Each syllable seemed to connect with the fire on a deeper level, twisting and dancing in sync as if the two were inherently linked.

The embers floated into the air. Most of them touched down on the stone floor of the quarry, dying out moments later. But some of them didn't fall. Some of the embers rose higher toward the sky.

A form began to emerge, coalescing out of nothing. The fiery embers merged with the darkness into something recognizable— a tall, dark figure. Its limbs sprouted slowly, forming legs, arms, a neck, a head. Its smoky tendrils assembled piece by piece as Tess continued her recitation without a pause.

Ally's gaze shifted back to Lucy, who lay motionless on the cold stone slab beside her. Nora was still clinging desperately to the girl, whispering in her ear and shaking her gently. Tears streamed down Nora's face.

"We have to go," Nora said.

Ally nodded without answering. The powerlessness gripped her chest. What were they supposed to do?

The form thickened into something almost solid, and all the ghastly details became clear. Its face formed last—two hollow sockets gaping where its eyes should be. Jagged, broken teeth filled its wide grin, and horns curled above its ears like charred roots. Its body writhed within a mass of burning soot and smoke that hovered above the ground.

It straightened its shifting form, and a stench filled the air. It was the same sickening smell of sulfur that she'd smelled at Nora's house.

Something began to fall around them—not snow from a Minnesota sky, but blackened flakes. Ash. It drifted off the demon's form and settled over everything—the ground, their clothes, their skin.

No doubt, this was the thing Daniel had seen in their house, except he'd only witnessed its shadow, its formless essence, without Tess's words to give it definition. He'd faced nothing but its raw horror. No wonder he'd been unable to describe it.

Tess repeated line after line of the text, and the demon materialized a little more each time. Her words were manifesting the thing into existence.

As the panic swelled, Ally fought the urge to turn and run. With no hope of escape, wasn't it better to take her chances with the ritual, to grab Lucy and flee as far and fast as she could before whatever evil had manifested in that space tonight caught up with them?

But it would catch up.

She was sure of that. There was no way out of this.

No way out.

Nora broke the tension by turning back to face Tess. She lifted the pistol and pointed it straight at the woman's chest. Tess didn't move. She didn't try to step out of the way, or even flinch. Instead, she stayed by her daughter's side, cradling Eve's head on her arm.

"I'll kill you!" Nora cried out.

"You would shoot a mother trying to save her daughter's life?" Tess spoke passionately.

Nora fired.

The first shot exploded against the stones behind Tess. Nora had missed—but the shot had visibly rattled Tess. The woman shuddered and now glared at Nora.

Nora fired again, this time clipping Tess's arm—the one that held her daughter—leaving a patch of torn cloth and a bit of blood oozing from the wound. The woman recoiled but turned her attention back to the demon. She continued reciting the lines louder and faster, with more intensity.

Ally grabbed Nora's arm, forcing her to lower the pistol. "No more."

Nora's eyes glistened with a dark intensity. "Don't stop me. I'll kill her."

"I know you will." She held out her palm. "Give me the gun."

Nora shook her head and instead turned the pistol toward the demon itself.

It approached them without hesitation.

Nora stood defiantly beside Lucy and fired two shots into the creature without effect. It never even flinched.

Ally pulled Nora back and grabbed the gun from her sister's hand. This wasn't something they could solve with a weapon of that kind. They needed a way to fight back, but how?

Instead of advancing toward them, it moved to the edge of the circle and leaned in toward Lucy's face. It stood only a few feet away from them, and the smell was nauseating. Ally held back the urge to vomit.

If it had wanted to pluck Lucy out of Nora's arms, it could have done so easily in that moment. It could have done anything it wanted.

Nora had swept her arms around Lucy, draping her own body over the girl to provide a last defense.

"Stay away from her!" Nora screamed.

Ally was ready to run, to grab Lucy in her arms and bolt out of the circle, knowing full well that they wouldn't survive—but it would be better for them to try. Better that she take her chances breaking the circle than die with that thing. She rushed forward and squeezed both Lucy and her sister at the same time. She wouldn't let that thing get to Lucy, not under any circumstances. There had to be a way to fight back, or at least delay the demon long enough for them to escape.

Nora broke down and screamed, "No, no! Get away from her. This can't be happening."

The demon hovered in place, observing them, its gaze fixed on Lucy's little face on the slab. It turned away. Instead of grabbing Lucy, it turned back to Tess and Eve.

He approached the girl's wheelchair. Eve was slumped on her side, staring forward with dull eyes. Her mouth hung open, but she wasn't screaming.

Her mother seemed to offer her up to the demon like a gift.

"I've provided the sacrifice," she said. "Now save my daughter, as we agreed."

The demon glanced back at the statue beside the opening to the incinerator, noticing it for the first time. Then it extended its hand toward Eve's face, running its blackened fingers along her cheek and down to her chin. Her body tensed.

Tess smiled nervously. "Heal my daughter."

The form wavered in front of the girl for a moment, then broke apart just as it had formed, dematerializing and dispersing into thick black smoke. Instead of leaving them, it flowed into the girl's open mouth. She gasped and choked as it passed into her lungs.

Within moments, there was no sign that anything unnatural had stood before them. Eve sat motionless in her chair until her mouth clamped shut. It seemed the demon had kept his word. Eve became silent, at least still, for a long time. Then she swallowed, as if taking down a large piece of food.

At the same time, Lucy stopped breathing.

❧ 36 ❧

Ally's heart sank. It wasn't possible that Lucy was dead. But Lucy's lips turned blue, and her body went limp.

Nora flew into a panic. She swept her arms under Lucy, lifted her off the stone slab, and placed her on the ground within the circle. Kneeling beside the girl, she pressed into her daughter's chest with her hands shaking. "Breathe, honey! Come back to me!"

Ally tried to help—shaking Lucy again and again. What were the steps to perform CPR? She couldn't remember in that moment. "Please don't die, Lucy. Please don't die."

Nora maneuvered above her to the side while checking for signs of life. "She's dead," Nora cried. "She can't be dead! You can't be dead! Wake up, honey. Wake up!"

Tess called out somewhere behind them, "It's done. Ezeran has saved Eve's life!"

Ally turned back toward Tess, just as the woman had wrapped her arms around Eve. But instead of waking, her daughter convulsed. Something was wrong. Eve's eyes stretched wide open, and her face filled with terror. She shook in her chair, violently rocking from side to side, until she lurched forward and collapsed in her mother's arms.

Eve's eyes snapped shut, and she went still.

"No!" Tess shouted. "You can't leave me. Don't you dare leave me!"

She pulled her daughter into her chest and turned back to the incinerator. The flames still howled in the open space at the bottom.

"Help me, Ezeran," Tess cried. "Where are you? My daughter—"

Suddenly, Eve opened her eyes again and sat upright, pushing her mother out of the way. Tess's face showed astonishment—even joy—as her daughter glanced around with wide eyes.

Tess dropped to her knees. "Praise demon Ezeran! My Eve is whole again!"

Instead of embracing her mother, Eve knocked her backward and stood. A wide grin spread across her face while her mother trembled on the ground with joy. The girl wobbled for a moment until she stood on her own.

"Praise demon Ezeran," Tess cried out. "My Eve is healed. Finally, she is free again."

Eve took one step forward and scowled before clutching at her face. Digging her fingernails into her skin, she started pushing and pulling at the girl's flesh and hair. Within seconds, her face had changed to something unrecognizable. It shifted and bubbled, bulging out in unnatural ways.

Tess scrambled to reach her daughter. "What's happening? My Eve, what are you doing?"

Eve grabbed a handful of her cheek and arched back with her face toward the night sky. With a guttural moan, it pulled. The skin tore apart as she clawed at her flesh, ripping it away piece by piece. The bloody strands stretched with a thick wet sound like something being dragged through mud.

"This is what you provided for me to heal?" Eve screamed in a shrieking voice that sounded nothing like a young girl. "The vessel is broken. It cannot be fixed."

"No!" Tess cried, shaking her head. "You only need to work with her! My Ezeran, you are a god!"

Whatever had entered Eve's body didn't stop.

"You expect too much of me." The demon scoffed and cried out through Eve's body, "You misunderstood the pact."

"Then leave her!" Tess shouted. "I revoke my agreement."

"Do you think you get to decide how the pact is fulfilled?"

Tess pointed to Lucy. "Take *her* and leave my Eve in peace."

"What do you know about peace? I will take what I want!"

The demon continued its disassembly of Eve's face and hair, pulling the parts off one by one, leaving the eyes for last. It paused to observe each piece—staring at them with a grin as the blood sprayed off the girl's body.

"This is not worthy of my help," it growled. "But I will have my way. Let's see what we can do with this."

The voice boomed like an angry bull from the throat of such a small frame.

Tess stepped forward, clutching Eve with both hands. "You can't! Please! You can't have her!"

"Leave me!" it commanded.

Tess tried to pick up the pieces, scraping them off the ground and placing them on her daughter's bloody face. "Heal my Eve! You have the sacrifice." She gestured again toward Lucy. "I provided everything you asked. How can you do this to me?"

"Mother flame," the demon mocked, touching Eve's fingers to Tess's face. "You lit the fire. You fed me. Now burn. You can join your daughter forever in my home."

Tess recoiled as if something had struck her in the chest. She screamed, but it was cut short. Eve—the demon—grabbed her mother by the throat, lifting the woman into the air and holding her there, suspending her as she shrieked and gasped for air.

Ally caught sight of the statue from the corner of her eye. It was still lying on the ground not far from them. It had somehow righted itself, now standing up and facing her. It seemed to mock her now.

All along, it had guided the demon like a beacon in the night, and it was part of whatever was holding them there. Never protecting them. Never helping. Maybe she could still get to it, even from that distance. Break its power, like she should have done sooner.

Instinctively, she clutched the pistol she'd taken from Nora. Within a surge of rage and fear, she lifted the gun and aimed carefully at the thing's piercing black eyes.

She took one shot.

The statue broke apart, shattering in half.

A moment later, Lucy gasped—a shallow breath at first, and then another.

"She's breathing!" Nora cried out. "Lucy, honey—breathe."

Ally leaned in close to Lucy's face and also gasped in a breath.

Lucy's eyes opened. The girl's eyes sparkled in the light coming from the nearby flames. The color in her soft face had returned.

Ally grabbed Nora by the arm. "We have to get out of here. Now."

Nora stared back with wide eyes. "What about the circle?"

"It's broken." Ally nudged her to move.

Nora lifted Lucy again, clutching her tightly against her chest. The fear on Nora's face was gone, replaced now with determination.

They ran. Ally led the way. They made a clumsy, panting dash out of the circle and stumbled across the stone quarry toward the trees. Neither of them looked back—

Until Nora let out a piercing scream. Something thumped against the ground. When Ally glanced back, Lucy was lying on the ground, scrambling to stand again. Nora was clutching her arm, but Lucy was struggling to get away.

"She bit me!" Nora cried.

Lucy's face had changed. She looked more like an animal than a little girl. She clawed at Nora's arms, kicked at Ally's legs, then bolted back toward the circle and the horrific scene they'd just left behind.

"No!" Nora cried out.

"Lucy!" Ally screamed.

But the girl didn't seem to hear them. She didn't run like she had before, instead stumbling as she headed straight toward Tess. The woman was still struggling to keep the demon from tearing apart her daughter's body any further.

"Mother flame," Lucy cried out. "I'm ready. Here I am!"

$$\text{❧} \quad 37 \quad \text{☙}$$

Ally struggled to catch up with Lucy. The little girl was fast and determined, and Ally's shoes slipped across the loose rubble. Her heart pounded and her muscles burned as she pushed herself to the limit. Still, she couldn't catch up.

Nora was right beside her. She screamed, "Lucy, stop! Stop!"

Eve—the demon—released her mother when Lucy approached, and the woman crashed to the ground, choking and gasping for air. Eve—the demon—laughed, opening her arms wide as if to embrace the approaching child. "A better vessel," it said. "The pure one. The untouched. Just as promised."

"Yes," Tess said, coughing. "That's her. She's the true vessel. Take her and heal my Eve. There's still time. The little one is my gift to you. Please accept that girl as my sacrifice."

The candles Tess had lit burning brighter than ever as Lucy crossed over into the circle before anyone could stop her. A moment after she arrived beside Eve's mangled body, the flames burst higher around them, engulfing them like a cage. Lucy seemed oblivious to the danger and instead stretched out her welcoming arms toward the figure as if mesmerized.

Lucy's face glowed in the demon's presence. "I'm ready!"

"Lucy, come back!" Ally yelled.

Before Nora and Ally could pull Lucy away, the flames rose several feet into the night air and roared like a thousand voices screaming at once.

The heat scorched Ally's face, but she didn't stop. Instead, she headed straight into the fire. The wall of fire hit her with a blast of heat that flooded her body in searing pain. Her vision went black for a moment. She'd hit something unyielding, and it sent her tumbling backwards to the ground. Her elbows and spine cracked against the stone first, and another wave of pain flashed through her mind.

When she recovered, she looked down. Her clothes were on fire.

Nora rushed to put them out. She dropped to her knees and patted at the flames frantically. The flames had caught her shirt, but something else was burning.

Her hair.

Nora put that out too. The smoke engulfed them while she struggled to recover.

Ally tried to get up, but Nora pushed her back down and screamed at her. "Stay down!"

Rolling back and forth, as they'd taught her to do in school, Ally tried to help.

Nora was crying, on the edge of panic, but trying to hold it back.

A flood of emotions surged through Ally—guilt, fear, love. Her throat tightened, but she pushed away the thoughts for now and struggled to her feet.

Nora did the same, wiping away her tears. She glanced over Ally's body. "The fire's out."

Ally brushed off whatever ash had gathered on her smoldering shirt. The smoke filled her nostrils and lungs, and she coughed while turning back to the circle again.

Even her eyes ached. The smoke had clouded her vision, but she could still see Lucy was only a few feet in front of them. Still,

they had no way to reach her. They couldn't just pull her away—
her attention was fixed on Ezeran.

Nora cried out beside her—a cry that could only come from
a mother who had lost everything. She lurched forward, but Ally
threw her arm out.

"Wait," Ally said.

"I can't wait!" Nora pushed against her arm toward the
flaming barrier. "How can I just stand here?"

Ally didn't have an answer. They had almost escaped.

When Ally looked up, Lucy and Eve were embracing. Eve's
blood had smeared across Lucy's clothes and some of it blotted
her face. The two stood facing each other as if they'd known
each other their whole lives—like long-lost best friends, reunited
at last.

"My Eve." Tess reached up and grabbed Eve's hand, trembling
before her daughter on her knees. The blood soaking Eve's face
and clothes dripped down across Tess's hands. The woman's face
flooded with tears. "What has he done to you?"

A moment later, Eve convulsed, and the demon's shadowy
form poured out of Eve's mouth like black vomit. When the sickening mass finally disconnected from Eve's body, it collapsed in a
heap beside Tess. The shadowy form churned and hovered in the
air, its shape coalescing into something resembling the statue.

Tess screamed. She clutched her daughter's mangled body,
even after it hit the stone ground, and struggled in vain to save
her life.

Lucy stood reverently beside the demon with her face down.

The demon gestured to Eve's now disfigured body lying
motionless on the ground a short distance away. "We will dispose
of that body instead."

Despite Eve's ghastly injuries, the girl's chest was still rising
and falling.

"No," Tess cried out. "That's not what we agreed!"

"You offered the girl's blood to Moloch—"

"For healing," Tess said in a weak voice. "That was the pact."

"You made the pact," it said. "He merely signed it in your child's blood."

Tess crumpled beside Eve's broken body, desperately trying to mend the discarded pieces of flesh that the demon had torn away. Some of them were stained with the ash that had fallen from the incinerator. She patched the girl's bleeding form, even as the demon seemed to turn his focus back to Lucy.

The demon caressed her face. "This one will survive... serve my purposes."

Tess tugged at her daughter's clothes, while still holding her hand. "She doesn't deserve this, Ezeran. *I* don't deserve this. You can't let my daughter die. *I* brought you here."

"Yes, you did." He kept his back to her. "You did well, and you'll get your reward."

"I only want my daughter."

The demon grinned. "You can have that... thing. I'm done with it."

"No..." Tess shook her head. Eve's blood dripped over the woman's hands and down her arm. "She won't survive."

"You can stop this!" Ally cried out to Tess.

Even through the woman's desperation, Ally couldn't help but see herself reflected in her. It was all the same betrayal, the same manipulation, the same twisted path the demon had used on both of them. The madness had to end—now. "You have to break its power—it's the only way. Don't you understand?"

Tess shook her head while tears streamed down her cheeks. "It's too late."

"It's not," Ally pleaded. "You can't let this happen."

The woman wilted further until lifting one hand to the center of her buttoned shirt. In a swift, stubborn motion, she ripped her shirt open and crawled closer to her daughter's side. Leaning in so her lips almost touched her daughter's cheek, the woman whispered in her ear. A moment later, she reverently gathered some of her daughter's blood in her palm and dipped one finger in it. She touched her bloody finger against her bare chest and drew a bloody sigil. It was the same symbol she'd drawn on Lucy earlier.

Without turning back toward Tess, the demon taunted her. "You're not a worthy vessel. If you think that even for a moment..." He laughed. "I don't need you anymore."

"Take me," Tess cried out. "Leave my daughter."

"Leave this? Yes. I will take you too... and then the girl. See? I will have all of you."

The demon's form straightened and drifted out of the fiery circle. It glided across the ground toward Tess in a nightmarish advance like a predator stalking its prey, while leaving Lucy behind. The girl didn't move. She stood in the same spot, but her eyes were wide open. Her gaze was locked on the flames roaring inside the mouth of the incinerator.

"Lucy!" Nora cried over and over. "Please get out of there!"

Lucy didn't seem to hear.

When the demon reached Tess, it flooded into the woman's open mouth within seconds. She bolted upright and jumped to her feet, standing erect and strong—just as Eve had done after becoming possessed. Her body wavered as the demon struggled to control it.

Tess screamed, a mix of woman and monster. Her face contorted, shifting between grotesque and betrayal, and then she stepped toward the incinerator. Clawing at her face, she let out another groan, a guttural cry of tortured pain, moving forward like a newborn learning to walk.

She paused to glance back at Lucy with sadness in her eyes, then turned her gaze down at Eve's bloody and broken body. The girl's chest had stopped rising and falling. "Sleep, my darling."

The next moment, Tess charged headfirst into the mouth of the incinerator. She sped up toward it with her hands curled into fists above her chest, then tossed herself into the heart of its raging flames.

Screams filled the air—Tess's anguished cries rising above the demon's furious moans—all coming from the same throat.

At the peak of the incinerator's brightest flames, Lucy seemed to snap out of whatever had come over her. The circle's barrier of fire also fell away. The flames collapsed to simple candlelight for a moment before finally flickering out.

Lucy turned to them, her face tired and full of confusion. "Mommy? Where am I?"

Nora jumped forward into the circle and embraced her daughter. "You're safe. I'm right here."

Ally tugged on her sister's arm. The stench of death still filled the air.

Nora and Lucy followed her away from the circle, but they paused after they were a safe distance from the tragedy.

Ally glanced back and stared at Eve's mangled body lying in a pool of blood beside her wheelchair. The girl's hand was slick with blood. It was still stretched out to where her mother had sat huddled beside her in her final heartbreaking moments.

The sound of sirens filled the air.

✵ 38 ✵

Nora held Lucy's hand while leading her away from the circle. Daniel came crashing out of the trees a moment later, surrounded by four uniformed police officers with their weapons drawn. The officers scanned the quarry with their over-sized flashlights, pausing with wide eyes and gaping mouths on the horrific scene in front of the incinerator.

The lead officer moved in front of the others and called out, "Sheriff's Department. Stay where you are. We're here to help."

Daniel rushed ahead, past the officers, straight toward them. He embraced Nora first, holding her for several seconds before his gaze dropped to Lucy. He embraced her for even longer, with his eyes full of tears. The three of them stood like that with their arms around each other, with Lucy huddled between them.

Two officers broke away toward the incinerator. Their radios crackled as they called in the scene. Another officer hurried to Eve's wheelchair, where the girl's body lay on the ground where the demon had discarded her. Kneeling, the officer gently rolled her onto her back, pressed two fingers against her throat, and after a long moment, gave a subtle shake of his head to his colleague.

The lead officer arrived beside them. "Detective Harris, Sheriff's Office," he said again. "We've got medics on the way. Just stay calm and let us secure the scene."

He turned his focus back to the incinerator, sweeping his flashlight over the flames that still poured from its mouth around Tess's charred body.

"Damn," he said under his breath.

Tess's lower body dangled out. Her upper body was unrecognizable. Whatever fuel Tess had used to ignite the old incinerator still burned with a voracious appetite.

Detective Harris spoke into his radio. "Dispatch, we're going to need fire rescue at the quarry. Get Engine 14 down here. Copy?"

Daniel leaned down to Lucy. "Are you okay?"

The girl nodded but kept silent.

Ally slipped her arm around Lucy and shifted herself sideways to block Lucy's view of the carnage behind them.

Shame and relief filled Nora's heart. Her sister had only acted out of love. She turned to face Ally. "You were right."

A pained expression flashed across Ally's face. "I let you down."

Daniel shook his head while staring at the ground. A moment later, he looked up and met her gaze. "I won't ever doubt you again."

Detective Harris shifted to the other side of them. He spoke calmly but professionally. "You're safe now. Paramedics are on the way. Just stay with me. Anyone hurt?"

Nora shook her head. "Not physically."

The detective kept glancing back at the incinerator. "I saw what happened on my way down through the trees. If I hadn't seen it for myself..."

"She planned to kill Lucy," Nora said.

He nodded but didn't seem to hear her. His gaze was fixed on Tess's gruesome remains hanging from the incinerator. "The damndest thing I've ever seen."

EMTs arrived a short time later with two stretchers. They

went to Eve first, crouching beside her, but quickly confirmed what the officer had already indicated—she was dead. One of them pulled a sheet from his bag and gently laid it across Eve's face before walking over to Lucy.

"Let me see her," the EMT said softly.

Nora stepped out of the way but still held her daughter's hand as the EMT inspected the bloody marks across her chest, carefully lifting her pajama top to check for any wounds.

"Nothing serious," he said. "It's surface level, but we should get her cleaned up and have another look."

Lucy turned her head toward Nora, her face full of confusion. "She told me she was taking me to Heaven, Mommy. I don't remember... How did I get here?"

Nora stroked her daughter's hair. She fought to hold back her tears. "It's better that you don't remember, honey. She tried to steal you from me, sweetheart. But she's gone now. You're safe."

Lucy's lips trembled. "I'm sorry."

Nora shook her head. "You don't have anything to be sorry about. She was a bad woman. We'll go home soon."

The officer standing nearby lowered his notepad. "We'll need to get her statement," he said, "but not now."

"She needs to go home," Daniel added.

The detective nodded. "She can go."

"Can *we* go?" Ally asked.

"Not yet."

Nora gave her daughter one last hug before Daniel led Lucy away. He guided her away from the scene but glanced back briefly at the edge of the trees. Nora met his gaze for a moment. Even from that distance, she could see something had shifted in his eyes. The night had changed him forever too. Then he turned away and continued leading Lucy up the hill toward the flashing lights.

"We'll need to get your statements first," the detective said.

Another officer arrived and separated her from Ally. Nora was led away to the edge of the trees while Ally stayed behind with the detective. The officer took down her side of the story, and she told him everything—everything he would believe, anyway—leaving out any mention of demons. She hoped Ally was doing the same, avoiding any talk of their involvement with the occult. It would be difficult enough to explain everything without bringing their background into the equation.

While giving her statement, she watched one of the officers bend down and stare at the bloody knife Tess had used to cut Eve's wrist. It was lying beside Eve's wheelchair. He leaned toward it for a moment, glanced back at Eve, then walked away.

He stepped over to the pistol next—and she shivered. She had fired it at Tess, one of the rounds clipping the woman's shoulder. Nora hadn't killed anyone, but things might have turned out very differently if she had succeeded in killing the woman. They would be charging Nora with murder right now.

The officer followed Nora's gaze to the revolver and asked, "Did someone fire the gun?"

"Yes," Nora admitted. "I shot it—three times. I shot her in the arm, just to stop her."

He wrote everything down without commenting. "Who does it belong to?"

"My sister, but I had it in my purse."

"Why did you have it in your purse?"

"Self defense."

He nodded. More notes. "Did she fire it?"

"Yes, at the statue."

The officer looked up. "The statue?"

"Tess was using it for some sort of ritual," Nora said. After I dropped the pistol, Ally used it to shoot the statue. She was trying to disrupt Tess long enough for us to escape. Tess intended to kill Lucy.

"Do you have a motive?" the officer asked.

"No," Nora said. "It's hard to understand why anyone would do something like this?"

The officer nodded but continued with another barrage of

questions about how everything had unfolded. Nora relayed the horrific events, while swallowing her emotions at any mention of Lucy. Finally, he put away his notepad and led Nora back to the detective and Ally.

When they were reunited, the detective also put away his notes.

"Are we free to go?" Ally asked.

"Normally," he said, "we'd ask you to come with us downtown to fill in all the details. But after what I saw—" He glanced back toward the incinerator. "—there's no need. We'll keep in touch."

Nora nodded. More officers arrived during their questioning. A flurry of camera flashes lit up the night as they captured all the gruesome details and marked everything. They were joined a short time later by a fire crew, who taped off the scene and shut down the incinerator's fire with great difficulty after removing Tess's body.

The detective finally agreed to let them go an hour after Daniel and Lucy had gone home. By then she was beyond exhausted and just wanted to get back to her family.

Nora led Ally up the hill, following the same path they had taken on their way down. They didn't say a word as they trudged back to their cars, but before climbing into her car, Nora met her sister's gaze. She smiled, if only to say thank you, and her sister smiled back.

After climbing into her car, Nora closed the door and switched on the engine.

A flood of emotions broke through all at once, and she cried.

Nora carried the broken statue in her purse. She'd asked the police for the shattered pieces once their investigation was over, and they'd provided them a few weeks later. It wasn't easy to hold them in her pocket now, as she sat in the front pew of St. Michael's Catholic Church with her family. This broken statue had nearly destroyed her family. But she was determined to make sure someone disposed of it properly.

Lucy was sitting between her and Daniel, with Ally on the outside edge. They were alone in the sanctuary while Father Tony stood in front of them, preparing a blessing for Lucy. He'd invited them to arrive before the other parishioners in the morning. They would need the extra privacy to deal with everything without attracting unwanted attention.

The father had prepared everything. He was dressed in his vestments and held a silver basin of holy water in one hand and a Bible in the other.

They'd purchased a new dress for Lucy the previous day. Lucy had picked it out. A plain white dress with a small ribbon at the waist. Nothing fancy, but she looked almost angelic in it, and she beamed with pride. It was the first formal dress they'd ever purchased for her.

The bloody mark Tess had painted onto Lucy's skin was long gone. They had washed it away in the tub the same night after they'd gotten home from the quarry. The events of that night still rattled her. She couldn't shake the fear that something might still have lingered behind, like it had with Blanco.

That's why they had come—to make sure Lucy was safe.

After a quiet moment, Father Tony gestured for Lucy to stand. She handed Blanco to Ally, who gathered the purring cat in her arms. Lucy stepped forward, with the morning sunlight catching the edges of her white dress. She looked angelic for a moment—radiant—much more than just their sweet little girl.

As Lucy stood before him, Father Tony held out his hand and dipped his fingers into the holy water he'd blessed in front of them earlier. He traced a cross on Lucy's forehead. A bead of water dripped down her nose. She scrunched her face at the same time and wiped it away before anyone could stop her.

"You've walked through a lot of darkness," he said. "But today we seal you in light. No longer are you bound to anything beyond this world. I bless you in the name of the Father, and of the Son, and of the Holy Spirit. May His hand never leave you."

Then he stepped back, made the sign of the cross over his chest, and turned to Nora.

"Do you have the statue?"

"Yes." She tapped the edge of her purse.

He nodded. "Then, let's finish this."

Leading them outside through the back door, Father Tony headed toward the cemetery behind the church.

Nora walked with one arm over Lucy's shoulders and the other hand over her purse. Ally carried Blanco, and the cat seemed content in her arms.

The cemetery had been there for a long time, judging by the dates on the gravestones. Some of them dated back to the 1800s. It stretched out no more than a few hundred feet in each direction, with rows of weathered crosses and marble markers leaning at odd angles, but they had packed a lot of plots in that small space.

They walked all the way to the back and then circled around behind an old oak tree. Despite its age, the branches were flush with leaves, and newly formed acorns were sprouting everywhere. Father Tony stopped and turned back to them while staring down at a shallow hole that someone had already prepared. It was only a few inches across, but clearly deep enough to hold what they had brought to bury forever.

After they'd gathered around the small pit, he gestured toward the space around them.

"This is sacred ground," he said. "Father Elias Whitmore planted this tree more than a century ago. He blessed it then, and its roots will bind whatever we bury here forever."

Nora dug the jagged stone shards out of her purse and crouched in front of the hole. Dropping each piece inside one at a time, her body warmed and her surroundings brightened. Or maybe that was just the sun coming out from behind a cloud.

In either case, she wiped her hands and stood again. "Good riddance."

"May this never see the light of day again," Father Tony said, producing a vial of holy water from his pocket and sprinkling it over the hole. "Ashes to ashes, stone to dust."

A pile of dirt sat next to the hole. Lucy bent down and scooped up a handful of soil before tossing it in. Nora joined her, throwing in the dirt with more force than necessary, and slowly, the hole started to fill.

As the dirt fell over the broken stones, they didn't look like stones anymore. For just a fleeting moment beneath the soil, they looked like someone's face. Someone she recognized instantly. The pale, wide-eyed face of a girl staring up from the darkness.

Lucy's face.

Nora gasped.

But then it was gone.

"Something wrong?" Daniel asked, his voice full of concern.

The stones were just stones again.

"No," Nora said. "It's just..." *...my imagination playing tricks on me.* "It's nothing."

Lucy lunged forward a moment later and shoved the last of the dirt into the pit. She laughed while sealing the thing into the ground. She even stomped on it with her foot again and again.

Nora didn't stop her.

Her shoes were getting dirty. Daniel pulled her away. "That's enough."

A noise came from above them. Glancing up, Lucy laughed again. A squirrel was scurrying across one of the low branches.

"He's watching us." Lucy pointed at him. She picked up an old, dried acorn off the ground and held it up toward the squirrel. "Come and get it."

Nora moved between them and nudged her away. "Don't feed him," she said. "We don't need any more pets."

Lucy dropped the acorn.

They headed back toward the church in silence. Stepping out of the cemetery, a wave of relief swept through Nora. That was it. The statue was gone. Lucy was safe. And somehow, they had survived a twisted, dangerous woman's attempt to kill their daughter. She never wanted to look back.

Still, she glanced over her shoulder... to make sure.

Nothing had changed. The hole was still packed with dirt. The squirrel was gone.

"Something wrong?" Father Tony asked.

She shook her head and continued forward. "Let it all rest in peace."

The Dark Covenant series continues here with The Last Demon: Dark Covenant Series Book 3! Available now!

Read more by Dean Rasmussen on Amazon.com!

PLUS, get a **FREE** short story at my website!

www.deanrasmussen.com

★★★★★
Please review my book!

If you liked this book and have a moment to spare, I would greatly appreciate a short review on the page where you bought it. Your help in spreading the word is *immensely* appreciated and reviews make a huge difference in helping new readers find my novels.

The Last Séance: Dark Covenant Series Book 1
The Last Medium: Dark Covenant Series Book 2
The Last Demon: Dark Covenant Series Book 3

Shine House: An Emmie Rose Haunted Mystery Book 0
Hanging House: An Emmie Rose Haunted Mystery Book 1
Caine House: An Emmie Rose Haunted Mystery Book 2
Hyde House: An Emmie Rose Haunted Mystery Book 3
Whisper House: An Emmie Rose Haunted Mystery Book 4
Temper House: An Emmie Rose Haunted Mystery Book 5
Raven House: An Emmie Rose Haunted Mystery Book 6
Amber House: An Emmie Rose Haunted Mystery Book 7

Dreadful Dark Tales of Horror Book 1
Dreadful Dark Tales of Horror Book 2
Dreadful Dark Tales of Horror Book 3
Dreadful Dark Tales of Horror Book 4
Dreadful Dark Tales of Horror Book 5
Dreadful Dark Tales of Horror Book 6
Dreadful Dark Tales of Horror Complete Series

Stone Hill: Shadows Rising (Book 1)
Stone Hill: Phantoms Reborn (Book 2)
Stone Hill: Leviathan Wakes (Book 3)

ABOUT THE AUTHOR

Dean Rasmussen grew up in a small Minnesota town and began writing stories at the age of ten, driven by his fascination with the Star Wars hero's journey. He continued writing short stories and attempted a few novels through his early twenties until he stopped to focus on his computer animation ambitions. He studied English at a Minnesota college during that time.

He learned the art of computer animation and went on to work on twenty feature films, a television show, and a AAA video game as a visual effects artist over thirteen years.

Dean currently teaches animation for visual effects in Orlando, Florida. Inspired by his favorite authors, Stephen King, Ray Bradbury, and H. P. Lovecraft, Dean began writing novels and short stories again in 2018 to thrill and delight a new generation of horror fans.

ACKNOWLEDGMENTS

Thank you to my wife and family who supported me, and who continue to do so, through many long hours of writing.

Thank you to my friends and relatives, some of whom have passed away, who inspired me and supported my crazy ideas. Thank you for putting up with me!

Thank you to everyone who worked with me to get this book out on time!

Thank you to all my supporters!